D1270596

Slay Fell Things

CLAW & WARDER

Episode 9

ERIK HENRY VICK

RATATOSKR PUBLISHING

NEW YORK

RATATOSKR PUBLISHING
2080 NINE MILE POINT ROAD, UNIT 106
PENFIELD, NY 14526

PUBLISHER'S NOTE: THIS IS A WORK OF FICTION. NAMES, CHARACTERS, PLACES, AND INCIDENTS ARE A PRODUCT OF THE AUTHOR'S IMAGINATION. LOCALES AND PUBLIC NAMES ARE SOMETIMES USED FOR ATMOSPHERIC PURPOSES. ANY RESEMBLANCE TO ACTUAL PEOPLE, LIVING OR DEAD, OR TO BUSINESSES, COMPANIES, EVENTS, INSTITUTIONS, OR LOCALES IS COMPLETELY COINCIDENTAL.

SLAY FELL THINGS/ ERIK HENRY VICK. -- 1ST ED.
ISBN 978-1-951509-11-8

Table of

Contents

In memory of my grandfathers,
Henry M. Vick and Herbert G. Meyer,
who would have loved this story.

I hope you enjoy *Slay Fell Things*. If so, please consider joining my Readers Group—details can be found at the end of the last chapter.

CHAPTER I

THE BODY

In the magical justice system, magically based offenses are considered bad form.

In the Locus of New York, the dedicated teams of supernatural detectives who investigate these breaches of Canon and Covenants are members of an elite squad known as the Supernatural Inquisitors Squad.

These are their stories.

I

Dee Dolosic grimaced and turned her back to the arctic blast of wind pouring down on her from the ballfields near the North Woods of Central Park. The naked trees frowned down on her as she walked between them, and the gray morning sky peeked through the leafless branches arching above her head, but she didn't look up at it. She didn't know if she suffered from Seasonal Affective Disorder, but she knew for certain she didn't like gray skies. She crossed under the 102nd Street Crossing via the Springbanks Arch and headed into the denser forest around The Loch, hoping to block out at least some of the ugly sky. Winter in Manhattan came far too soon for Dee's tastes.

She had a walking date with her bestie, Liz Willnow, but she found herself hoping that Liz would be late. She needed the time to work her way through her dark mood. That's why she'd come to the park early, why she'd chosen to walk through the ballfields instead of going straight to Glen Span Arch where they'd agreed to meet.

She bent and scooped up a ball of snow and began to strip away the orange and yellow leaves still clinging to it. Fall was so pretty in New York, but at the end of it, winter loomed, and she *hated* the cold. She *hated* the snow.

"There you are!"

Dee lifted her gaze, a smile already plastered to her face. "You're early, Liz," she called.

"Yeah, yeah. You've known me seventeen years, girlfriend. And more to the point, I've known *you* seventeen years. Do you think I can't hear the blues in your voice?"

She glanced down at the snowball in her hand and let it fall. She sighed and lifted her shoulders. "Well..."

"Yeah, yeah. Winter's here. I know." Liz stepped to her side and shoved her arm into the crook of Dee's. "You can't control the seasons, dear."

"I could move."

Liz nodded. "Sure. And if I hadn't heard you say the same thing for the last sixteen winters, I might be worried."

"Let's get off the path," said Dee. "I don't want to run into anyone."

"This is a city of eight million people, dear. The chances of coming across anyone we know are—"

"That's what you said the day we bumped into those creepy IT guys from work."

Liz chuckled. "Touché. Lead on, oh intrepid explorer of wooded areas."

Dee turned off the path and strolled underneath the boughs, kicking small drifts of snow as she went. "How's the man?" she asked after a few moments of silence.

"Oh, you know. He's getting ready to watch the game."

"You mean it takes more than plunking down on the sofa and picking up the remote?"

Liz's laughter rang through the trees. "Girl, you have no idea. He's decided that he needs to paint his face this year."

"Oh, he's going to the games in person?"

"No."

"Then...a party or something?"

Liz's smile stretched. "No. He watched last week's game in his boxers and his Giants jersey with a painted face."

"And...only you saw him?"

"You're getting the picture, now."

"But..."

"Don't strain your brain, Dee. It makes no sense unless you are a rabid football fan."

Dee shook her head and grinned. She kicked another pile of snow, then looked down at it when her foot hit something solid. "Ouch."

"Tree root?" asked Liz.

"I don't think so...it's smooth." She brushed the toe of her shoe through the pile again and gasped as she exposed a weathered gray heel embedded in the damp earth.

"Is that..." Liz shivered.

Dee nodded, already calling the police.

2

Dru pulled the Crown Vic across the lane of oncoming traffic in the 102nd Street Crossing and onto the concrete path. She sighed as she put the car in park. "It's an old body, Leery."

"Hey, at least it isn't an old body in the dead of the night," said Leery. "At least there's no fog." He reached for his *trenta* of Starbucks coffee, took a sip, then got out. "Where'd they say to go?"

"Through the Springbanks Arch, then follow the crime scene tape."

Leery grunted. "Nothing like a morning stroll through nature." He led her down the path decorated with sprinkles of fresh snow and turned to follow another through the arch. "At least we found a parking space close by."

"You mean the path where I parked the car?"

"Exactly, Dru. Glad you're finally coming around to see things my way."

She chuckled and bumped him with her shoulder.

"Before we get to the scene, Dru, let's get something straightened out."

"Sure, Leery."

"I'm better now. Everyone says so."

"Everyone, eh?"

"The feedings have done wonders. Your mother said so."

"Ah."

"And Luci said—"

"I'm still taking lead, Leery," she said in a quiet, though firm, voice.

"Yeah, and I'm okay with that. What I'm saying is—"

"'Whatever you say, Dru.' That's what you're saying."

"Um...I—"

"That sounds remarkably *unlike* 'Whatever you say, Dru.'" She stopped walking and turned to face him.

"Well, the thing I wanted—"

Dru cocked her fist on her hip and tilted her head to the side.

"Uh, I'm having a hard time telling if you're joking or not."

She narrowed her eyes, and for a split-second, they blazed with red light.

Leery took a swig of coffee and turned his attention to the arch. "What I meant—"

She flattened her lips.

"I'm better, Dru. Not one hundred percent, I'll give you that, but close enough. You take the lead, I'm fine with that. All I'm saying is—"

Dru stomped her foot.

"Whatever you say, Dru. That's all I'm saying."

"That's what I thought," she said with a smile. She turned and walked into the shadow of the arch. "You coming?" she called over her shoulder.

3

Five minutes later, they stood outside the area marked off by crime scene tape. A man wearing sergeant's stripes, with a salt-and-pepper beard and wire-rim glasses had the log duty, and when he saw Leery coming, he grinned a little, then hid it with a grimace and popped his earbuds out.

"They let you out of the precinct?" asked Leery by way of a greeting.

"Yes, they wanted a real cop out here." The sergeant had a mild English accent.

"Hey, Dru, meet Ben Aaronovitch. Never ask him for directions. He thinks this is London."

"Don't listen to him, my dear," said Ben, extending his hand.

Dru lay her hand in his upturned palm. "Dru Nogan. Pleased to meet you, Sergeant Aaronovitch."

"Did I mention he's a wizard? Or are you still an apprentice, Ben?"

Ignoring Leery, Ben bent over her hand and brushed his lips against her knuckles. "The pleasure is all mine, and you must call me

Ben." He glanced at Leery. "Who did you piss off to draw this lout as a partner?"

"Jealousy is so ugly, Aaronovitch," said Leery with a grin.

"Not half so ugly as you, my friend."

Leery took the clipboard from under Ben's arm and scrawled his name on it. "Yeah, yeah," he murmured. "Now, if you can let go of my partner's hand..."

"Oh, yes," said Ben with a blush.

Dru smiled and took the clipboard. She signed her name and handed it back to him. "Thank you, Sergeant."

"What are we walking into, Ben?" asked Leery.

Aaronovitch frowned. "Someone staked a vampire, Oriscoe. Someone planted him like a tree."

"Staked and buried head-down in the woods?" Dru asked with a frown.

"Indeed," Ben said. "Whoever did the deed did not want him to return."

"That's cold," said Leery.

"Well, it *is* winter."

"Har-har, Aaronovitch. Leave the corny jokes to a professional. Like me."

Leery and Dru ducked under the tape and walked toward the cluster of people standing in a loose knot toward the center of the marked-off space. The technicians from the ME's office had already exhumed the body, and a wooden stake pinned the dead vampire through the chest.

"Do you recognize him?" asked Dru, walking closer. The remains seemed mummified, desiccated. The wooden stake driven through his chest was carved and marked with runes.

"Is that LaSalle?" asked Leery.

"I think so."

Leery pointed at the stake. "Runic magic?"

Dru glanced at him and nodded. "Yes. Some are Enochian, but I don't recognize the others. I'll give you odds they are specific to Dead Set rituals."

"What, retribution for the Gatsby thing? Why? LaSalle got away with it."

Dru shrugged. "Maybe he earned his stake for drawing too much attention to the organization."

"I could see that, I guess," said Leery. He squatted next to the corpse. "We'd better check his pockets."

"If it was the Dead Set, they wouldn't leave anything but the body behind," said Dru.

One of the ME's techs stepped closer. "Nothing on him," he said. "Except for the stake."

"Right, but that's more in him than on him," grunted Leery. "Send him to Liz Hendrix."

"That will not please her," said the tech. "She's out of the rotation this week. Court."

"Tell her Oriscoe sent him over," said Leery, waving him away. "Tell her we need her report sooner than possible. Tell her I said to use her magics." He made quote-fingers as he said the last word.

The tech arched an eyebrow. "You know that will only make her mood worse, right?"

"Nah. She loves me." Leery made shooing motions. "Now, run along and get this stiff processed." The tech rolled his eyes and turned away.

"Well, you haven't lost your way with people," said Dru.

"What? I said please."

"No, you didn't."

"I didn't?"

Dru shook her head.

"Well, I meant to. That counts, right?"

"If you say so," said Dru.

"Think if we get Hinton down here she can call up his spirit? I haven't hassled her enough this year, and I don't want to miss my quota."

"No," said Dru. "A vampire's soul is artificially bound to his flesh. Once staked, the spirit flees, ready to move on from this life. Few wait around to see if the stake will be removed."

"But still, she can summon—"

"No dice," said Dru. "Vampires are creatures of magic, Leery. LaSalle may have started life as a mundane man, but he spent centuries learning, growing. No one can force a vampire back to its discarded flesh."

"That's pretty inconvenient," said Leery. "You mean we're going to have to do actual police work?"

Dru dimpled. "Looks that way."

"That's pretty inconvenient," Leery repeated.

"We'll get through it," said Dru. "Somehow."

They made it as far as the Springbanks Arch before Dru's cell chirped. She pulled it out and glanced down at the phone, then stopped walking. Shaking her head, she said, "They need us back at the scene."

"Nah, that's just Aaronovitch. He probably wants your—"

"No, they found another one."

"Another body?"

"Another staked vampire."

"That's pretty inconvenient," Leery said with a sigh.

4

Leery stood gazing down at the sole of another gray, desiccated foot. One of the white-suited ME techs stood next to him, hands on his hips. Dru had the other techs clustered around her as she described the search pattern she wanted them to walk.

Leery sighed. "Run me through it again."

"Like I said, I was strolling around, looking for any evidence we might have missed—"

"I'd say another dead body qualifies," said Leery in a mild tone.

The tech frowned and looked at his feet. "Yeah. I tripped on it. There was a pile of snow—"

"Yeah, I get it," said Leery. He raised his gaze and swept the area with it, noting the frequent ripples of snow. "I guess we know what you and your friends will be doing today. I suggest snow shovels."

"Yes, and anyone you can spare."

"Oh, I can spare a lot of people," said Leery. "I want all the bodies to go to Hendrix."

"I don't think you understand how much she—"

"I get all that. But my gold shield says I don't have to care." Leery hit the tech with the stink eye. "At all."

"She might refuse—"

"Nah. Hendrix never met a dead guy she didn't like. Plus, she'll be interested in this. When was the last time you heard of a vampire getting staked and planted?"

"Well..."

"Damn right. Never in the past fifty years. This is unique." He looked back at the remains of Antoine LaSalle. "Well, you know what I mean."

The tech sighed. "Yeah." He turned his gaze up toward the gray sky. "She's going to kill me."

"Don't you worry," said Leery. "If she does kill you in a fit of rage, I'll make sure she gets away with it." He pointed to the mummified foot. "Let's get this vampire dug up." He turned and walked toward the police tape. "Aaronovitch!" he called. "Get on the phone to the precinct and get me some bodies. Well, *cops*. I've already got more bodies than I want."

5

Epatha Van Helsing appeared next to Leery as he and Dru watched the uniformed officers walking a grid inside the crime scene tape. So far, the body count was up to four, and none of them had ID.

"What a fifteen puzzle," she said, sweeping the scene with her gaze. "Whoever this is, he's sure swamped with enthuzimuzzy."

"You can say that again," said Leery with a nod.

"All decedents with long teeth?"

"So far, yes," said Dru. "Four of them."

"All staked, all buried head-down," said Leery.

"Well, that's the way you do it if you want them to stay where you leave them," said Van Helsing. "At least that's what my father used to say."

Dru cleared her throat. "This is going to be a mess, Lieu."

"That it is, chuckaboo." She nodded and turned away from the searching officers. "I understand we know the first one?"

"Yes," said Leery. "Antoine LaSalle."

"That skilamalink deserves nothing better," she said. "Just him, and it could be an affair of honor, but with all these other claret mug dampers..."

"Yeah," said Leery with a sigh. "A pattern."

"Don't even say what you're thinking, Oriscoe," said Van Helsing. "We'd better touch the ruffian behind this before the *pattern* grows much wider."

"We're on it, Lieu," said Dru.

"Do we have any notion how many beats our murderous cove has been at it?"

"No," said Leery. "I told the ME techs to route all the bodies to Liz Hendrix, though."

Epatha treated him to half a grin. "You're a daffy cussin, aren't you? Didn't that dragon give you enough of a batty-fang?"

"Think she'll be mad?" asked Leery.

"Never took you for a wooden spoon, Oriscoe. She's going to give you a big, fresh slice of mouth pie—right afore she shows you the daisy roots."

"Ah, well," he said. "The last time I died, it didn't turn out so bad."

Van Helsing grunted.

"Lieu," said Dru in a voice filled with uncertainty. "I know you don't want it said aloud, but I think the...size of this case merits—"

"Gorblimey, don't burst your stay-lace, Princess. We'll have us a fine taskforce in but a few moments of my return to the house." Epatha turned back to watch the searchers stomping through the snow. "Meantime, start finding out who all these peg tantrum fangers are."

"We're on it, Lieu," said Leery. "Come on, Dru. Nothing more we can do here. Let's go look into our old friend's recent doings."

CHAPTER 2

THE
INVESTIGATION

I

Dru let their cruiser idle up the street, her gaze stuck to the façade of Bevin Gemble-Croix's home. The curtains were pulled tight, and a sign hung from a thumbtack stuck in the door. A smaller sign covered the doorbell. "I wonder what that's about," she murmured.

Leery glanced at the building and frowned. "We'll probably find out. LaSalle's building looks locked up tight. Looks like a neighborhood canvass is in our future."

Dru glanced at the building and pursed her lips. "LaSalle's place never was all that welcoming," she said as her gaze zipped from one boarded up window to the next. "Well, might as well go ring the bell," she said as she parked the car and got out. "What's the worst that can happen?"

"A hundred vampires behind the door, waiting to spring out at us, and the signal is a ringing doorbell?"

"We're cops. Any vampires in there won't attack us, worry-wart."

"Yeah, you said something like that just before Dr. Agon set me on fire." He grinned, but Dru didn't. "Just kidding."

"You need to work on your material, jerk," she said. "Now, are you coming along, or should I do *all* the work myself?"

"Well, if you're offering..."

"Get your ass out of the car, Leery."

"Whatever you say, Dru."

"And they say you can't teach an old wolf new tricks." She grinned and gave him a little shove.

He got out of the car and came around to stand next to her. She bumped him with her shoulder, and he tried to hide his grin but failed.

They approached LaSalle's building, and Leery put his hand on her arm to stop her from ringing the bell. He lifted his chin and took a long sniff of the morning air.

"Something?" she whispered.

"Yeah, but I don't know what. It smells spicy... Like...cloves and cinnamon and mulled wine."

"He was an old vampire, Leery."

"Yeah, but it didn't smell this way before." He inhaled deeply through his nose. "And I smell animals."

"Animals? Wolves?"

"No, not wolves. Herbivores. Herd animals."

"None of that sounds very dangerous, Leery. And it *is* the holiday season. Maybe the neighbors made an effort to fill the street with pleasant Yuletide odors."

"Yeah, maybe." Leery turned his gaze back to the boarded-over windows, then scanned the leading edge of the roof. "But it doesn't feel that way. It's..."

"It's what?"

"Too quiet? Too..." He shook his head.

Dru squinted up at the roof, then shrugged. "I don't see anything."

"Yeah," said Leery. "Let's see what happens." He stepped up to the door and beat on it with his fist. "Open up in the name of the law!"

"Seriously?" asked Dru.

Leery shrugged and grinned at her. "I've always wanted to do that." They stood at the door, listening and waiting, for a handful of minutes, and then Leery beat on the door again. "NYPD!" he shouted. "I can hear you moving around in there!"

"Can you?" asked Dru in a whisper.

"As far as anyone else knows, yes."

"But not really?"

Leery turned his ear toward the door and narrowed his eyes. "I can't tell for sure. Something small, lightweight, maybe." He hitched his shoulders. "Could be rats." They waited a few more minutes, then he tried the knob and it turned. The door creaked open slowly, exposing the midnight shadows of LaSalle's hallway to the morning gloom. "Oh, spooky," said Leery with a grin. "NYPD!" he yelled again. "We're coming in unless you sing out and tell us not to." After half a minute, he glanced at Dru and shrugged.

"If there's a dragon in there, just run," she said.

"Whatever you say, Dru," Leery said through a one-sided smile.

"I'm going to regret that, aren't I?"

"My Magic 8 Ball says, 'it is certain.'"

"Does your Magic 8 Ball have any advice for walking with a limp?"

Leery mimed shaking the ball and looked down at his empty hands. "Ask again later."

"Well, does it say whether we should go inside or not?"

Leery squinted down the long dark hall. "It says, 'Cannot predict now.'"

"Wonderful. Some help you are."

Flashing a lupine grin, Leery pushed the door flat against the wall and stepped inside. "Let's go find out." He walked into the marble-tiled hall. "Got any light in that bag of tricks of yours, Dru-baby?"

Dru began a rune set and tsked. "Do you think if you have a limp in both legs it evens out into a regular walk?"

"I dunno."

"Keep up the lip, and you're going to find out."

"Promises, promises," Leery said with a wide grin.

Dru finished her set of pale gray runes and connected them with yellow lines. She muttered a word in the *Verba Patiendi* and then flung the runes above her head. Spinning like a top, the rune set drifted toward the ceiling, then burst into bright blue-white light.

"You make a pretty good flashlight, partner."

"Yeah, I bet you say that to all your girlfr—" Dru bit off the last syllable.

Pretending he didn't hear the slip, Leery turned and peered into the penumbra of shadow beyond the reach of the bluish-white light. The tiles were the same as before—red-streaked marble—but many had cracked, and some had gone missing altogether. Some of the ebony planks lining the walls hung loose, while others bore evidence of a fight, and someone had stripped away all of the gold trim. The crown molding remained pretentious and unharmed, though the matching chair rail hung askew in most places.

Leery crept down the hall, stopping at each doorway to peer into the rooms to the west of the hall. On their previous visit, all the doors save one had stood closed and locked, but no longer. Each room seemed functional but stripped of anything of value.

"Smell anything?" whispered Dru.

"Same as before, but it's weaker now that we're inside."

"Then—"

"Yeah, the scent probably came from the roof. Let's see if we can find a way up."

They cleared the first floor, finding only one staircase, which led to the second. It matched the first floor in the hallway running down the east wall of the building with rooms on the west, but the layout of the rooms was different. They passed a gigantic kitchen with the doors of its cabinets and giant Sub-Zero coolers standing open, an empty informal sitting room, a library stripped of its books, a bathroom, and what looked like a dressing room fit for a princess. At the front of the building, they found a spiral staircase leading up to the third floor, which served as LaSalle's personal living space. "Three ransacked floors," said Leery. "I'm sensing another pattern."

"Do you think whoever offed him did all this?" asked Dru.

Leery let his gaze rove around the empty bedroom, then shrugged. "I've seen stranger things."

"Yeah, me, too," said Dru. "Loved Millie Bobby Brown."

"Cute," said Leery.

"Yes, she is."

"Those are my jokes, you know."

"Finders keepers," said Dru with a shrug and a grin.

"Didn't like it as much as the first book in the series."

"Uh...you can read?"

"For Stephen King, I make the effort," said Leery as he turned away, so she didn't see his grin of triumph. "Come on, let's find the way up to the roof."

Following the pattern of the rest of the house, they had to walk the entire length of the floor to find the stairwell to the fourth floor, which was the attic. In the center of the floor, they found a metal ladder that led to a trapdoor set in the ceiling. Leery climbed up and put his hand flat against the door. He shook his head at Dru and undid the lock, then threw the trapdoor open. He climbed to the roof, then turned to help Dru up. "Nothing," he said.

"Is the odor still here?"

Leery sniffed and shrugged. "It's fading."

Dru surveyed the flat roof, arms akimbo, then shook her head. "Probably an innocent explanation."

"Do they still have those?" asked Leery. "I thought they went out with the hula hoop."

"Those are back, you know," said Dru.

"Why? Who would do something so evil?"

Dru shrugged. "The heart wants what it wants, I guess."

They turned and made their way back through the house down to the street. Leery closed the front door, then went to the car for some crime scene tape to drape across the stoop while Dru spun up a rune set to seal the door.

"I didn't see a crime scene," Leery said when they were done. "Not a murder scene, at least."

"Yeah," said Dru. "I think he disappeared for real at some point since the trial, and when that happened, his crew looted the place."

"Seems reasonable," agreed Leery, "but not very convenient."

"No."

"But, hey, if police work was easy, everyone could do it. Am I right?"

Dru's phone rang, and she answered it while she slid behind the wheel. "Oh, hello, Liz," she said.

A small grin blossomed on Leery's lips as he got in the passenger side.

"*Is your bastard partner with you?*" demanded Liz.

Dru glanced at him. "Yeah. He's right here beside me."

"*Punch him for me.*"

Dru balled up her fist and socked Leery in the shoulder.

"Hey!" he cried, his grin stretching to a smile.

"Done," said Dru. "Would you like to yell at him now?"

"*No. I'm not speaking to him.*"

"You don't have to. He's listening with those damn wolf ears of his. Just let rip. He'll hear it all."

"Imagine my surprise when I got back from my morning session of court. Just how many damn bodies did he send me?"

"No idea," said Leery in a loud voice. "They're still looking."

"Hit him again."

Dru punched Leery in the arm again.

"Harder. I didn't hear him squeal."

With a shrug, Dru complied.

"Ow!" said Leery. "I only sent them to you because you're the best, Liz! No one else could do this case justice!"

"Yeah, right. Put a sock in it, Oriscoe. If I wanted to talk to you, I'd have called your phone."

"Who gave you my number?"

"You did. About thirty-seven thousand times, remember? Back when you were trying to get into my pants?"

Dru cleared her throat and asked, "How many have arrived?"

"Five. So far."

"All vampires?"

"Unless the perp staked regular people for the fun of it."

"Ask her if she can ID any of them," whispered Leery.

"*And before Oriscoe opens his fat mouth, no, I haven't had time to ID any of them yet.*"

"What's she been doing?"

"*Preliminary external examination of the first couple of bodies shows what you saw at the scene. The enchanted stakes cannot be removed by conventional means. They appear to be the cause of...well, true-death. Until I figure out how to extract them—*"

"Is it likely that removing the stakes will allow us to contact the victims via a necromancer?"

The line hissed for a moment, then Liz cleared her throat. "*I don't believe so. The runes are a mix of Enochian and something else...something* old*...and they go further than making it difficult to remove the stakes. Until I can figure out what they are and get them translated, I won't know if the enchantment is responsible for the dissipated lifeforces of these victims, or if—*"

"Dissipated?"

"*Uh, yes. I may not have guessed the meaning of the runes correctly, however. I put in a request—*"

"Tell her we'll call Gonofrio to read them," said Leery.

"Did you hear that, Liz?"

"Yes. I appreciate it. Requests like this are often met with resistance from the Angelic Host."

Leery flipped out his cell and stared at it in confusion for a moment, then grinned and pressed the button to lock the screen again. With a sigh, Dru took it, swiped away the lock screen, and hit Gonofrio's contact before tossing it back. "We're on it," she said to Liz.

"Good. Listen, Dru, all of the victims are vampires. Maybe you should—"

"I'll be fine," said Dru. "Leery's back to almost full strength, and I have my own powers."

"Of course. I only mean that some of these victims appear to be ancient, even by the standards of your father's people."

"Thanks, Liz, but I'm more than vampire. And my family is always at my beck and call."

"Oh, sure. Be careful, just the same."

"I will."

"Now, I guess I'd better get done what I can before my afternoon *in court. Then, I can hurry back here and spend the night looking at the other staked vampires you guys dig up."*

"Sorry about that," said Dru. "But you really are the best woman for the job."

"*Yeah, thanks. Oh, Dru?*"

"Yes?"

"*Hit him again.*"

2

Leery hung up his phone, a puzzled grin on his face. He pressed what he thought was the lock button, then sighed and put the phone in his pocket with the screen still on. "You'd think no one could screw up a phone. I mean, it's a phone, right?"

"There, there," said Dru. She grinned as she turned the key in the ignition. "Is Vinny going to help?"

"Of course. He's a stand-up guy." Leery scratched his head. "You know, he keeps asking me about the Barghest."

"Yeah?"

"Hey, find a Starbucks, will ya? I'm dry over here. And yeah. He keeps asking if he's having a good time back home, if he's eating, if his packmates accepted him."

"Well, he did say he loves puppies."

Leery nodded. "Can you get me an update? I hate telling him I don't know anything."

"He could always ask my mother." Dru turned down Lex, ignoring a screech of tires and the blast of a cab's horn. "And so could you."

"You're really getting the hang of Manhattan driving," said Leery with a nod of approval. "But as for Vinny talking to your mother, I don't know. She really didn't seem to like him much."

"She was irked at him for being slow, that's all. I'm sure she's over it."

"Still. He's one of the Nephilim, and you know how sensitive they can be."

"Okay," said Dru. "I'll ask her." She pulled up in front of a Starbucks. "I'll have a tall, if you please."

"What, you want me to go in? I don't have the app thingy."

Dru grinned. "But you do have a mouth. We have ample evidence of that. Order like an old person."

"Yeah, I suppose I do owe you one or two."

"Two? Two hundred, maybe."

Leery shrugged and grinned but didn't move to get out of the car.

"You have to go inside, Leery."

"Oh, you're serious?"

"You must be a detective, Oriscoe."

"Whatever you say, Dru." He got out before she could punch him again. "While I'm gone, see if you can't solve this case."

Dru rolled her eyes and shooed him toward the door. "Seven sugars!"

"I know, I know. Ruined." Leery made it halfway to the door, then turned back, opened the door, and bent inside.

"No, honey, *you* pay."

"No, it's not that. Think we should call those Ceebies? They have resources the NYPD can't even dream about."

"Regina and Bryant? That's not a bad idea."

"Right," said Leery, sliding into the seat. "Just pull up on the sidewalk while you get the coffee." He pulled out his phone again and frowned at it.

"I knew it was too easy to convince you. You had this planned, didn't you?"

"Who? Me?" Leery batted his eyelids.

Still shaking her head, Dru bumped the car up onto the sidewalk and put it in park. "I could have called, you know."

"Nah. You don't know how to use my phone. Damn thing's persnickety." He scratched his head, then pressed the calendar icon and grimaced as his empty calendar appeared on the screen. "Now, why did that happen?"

With a chuckle, Dru took the phone and found the contact for Bryant Wheelbarrowx and dialed the number. "Here, genius," she said.

"See? It's troublesome, even for me."

"Yeah, yeah," she said. "How many?"

"*Trentas?*" He glanced down at the cupholder Wheelbarrowx had sent him. "It'll hold four."

3

Leery had started on the third giant cup by the time the Pepto Bismol pink Nissan Cube idled up next to them. The car had wide tires on black rims which necessitated flared wheel wells. It sat no more than half an inch off the macadam and had window tint so dark as to obscure who was driving. "Wow. The CBI must pay well for Regina to afford a car like that."

The window rolled down, showing Regina smiling in the passenger seat and Bryant leaning forward to see past her. "Can't you, for once, park in a normal place?" asked Wheelbarrowx.

"This *is* a normal spot," said Leery. "And Dru parked here, not me." He looked at Regina. "You are a trusting soul, aren't you?"

"What?"

"I mean, that looks like a custom job, and you let that guy drive it?"

She laughed and shook her head. "Because it's pink you think it belongs to me?"

"It doesn't?"

Bryant tipped him a wink. "I'll have you know that pink is a quite manly color. No soft-headed Sepo would dare drive it."

"If you say so. Next you'll be telling me pie and Pi are different things."

Bryant rolled his eyes. "Come on, Oriscoe. Let's find a lot where I won't scrape up my undercarriage."

"I'm going to leave that one alone, Wheelbarrowx. Too easy. Anyway, you sure pink is a manly color?" Bryant opened his mouth, but Leery waved him off. "Follow us…if you can." He looked at Dru. "Hit it."

Dru turned her head toward Bryant, revved the engine, and dropped it into gear, leaving giant smoking elevens down the sidewalk. Looking in the rearview mirror, Dru frowned. "Too much?"

"Nah. I'd call that perfect."

Dru slid around the corner onto West 42nd Street and slammed the accelerator to the floor. Leery hunched forward and peered in the side view mirror, grinning as the pink abomination came screeching around the corner. "Where is this park?" Dru asked.

"Up past Fifth. It'll be on the left. Behind the library."

Dru blipped the siren to cut through the red light at Madison, then smirked at Leery. "That'll get him." She gunned it and raced through the yellow at Fifth Avenue, then took her foot off the accelerator and let the Crown Vic coast past the library.

"You done good, partner," said Leery as the cruiser rolled past the subway station. "Park anywhere along here on the left."

Dru glanced at him a moment, then shrugged and pulled across the oncoming lanes and headed for the red swatch painted down the outside lane.

"Oh, not in the bus lane, Dru," said Leery, feigning shock.

She wagged her eyebrows at him then bumped the car up onto the wide sidewalk between a lamp post and a pair of poles set in the concrete. She inched the car close to a red pole and killed the engine. "Is that close enough to the hydrant?"

"Well, if they'd get rid of those stupid posts you could get closer, but as things are, you're fine."

They got out and met at the rear of the vehicle, both adopting a "patiently waiting" pose and leaning against the trunk. "Think I lost him?" asked Dru.

"Nah. Those Ceebies are experts at navigation and stuff like that. He's just taking his sweet time. Probably wants to make an entrance. You know how those Aussie vampires can be."

Dru grunted a laugh, then jerked her chin at the pink vehicle threading its way past the library. "There he is."

"See? What did I tell you," said Leery as Bryant guided the car onto the wrong side of the road, waving and smiling at the cabbies honking their horns at him. "Always have to be the center of attention. You watch. He'll have on some crazy getup. MC Hammer pants or something like that."

Wheelbarrowx pulled the bubblegum-colored Cube onto the sidewalk with exquisite care and pulled up behind them. He and Regina got out and walked over to the Crown Vic. "I see he's ruined you as a driver, Princess."

"None of that," said Dru. "You know my name."

Bryant hitched his shoulders, making the hem of his sassy fur coat flap around his thighs in the light breeze. Underneath the coat, he wore black. He'd exchanged his short-sleeved black T-shirt for one with long sleeves, and they stuck out four inches past the cuffs of his fuzzy coat sleeves. He turned to Leery. "Was this park your bright idea?"

"What, Bryant Park?" said Leery with half a grin.

"Don't mind him," said Regina. "He's been testy since the body shop put the wrong color on his baby here." She flashed a blood-red smile at Dru. "Hi, Dru."

"Hello, Regina. How's life at the Bureau?"

"Can you believe they won't let me wear my piercings?" grumped Bryant. "Bloody travesty, that is."

Regina gave him a backhanded swat. "She was asking me, you drongo." She grinned at Dru. "It's not as exciting as UC work, but we're a little high-profile for that now. The bosses don't quite know what to do with us." She wore the same black leather trench coat trimmed in hot pink faux fur as the day they'd met, but underneath she wore a white button-down shirt over black dress slacks and black leather boots with four-inch heels.

"So, the color was a mistake, Wheelbarrowx?" asked Leery. "What color did you want?"

Bryant grunted. "How's that cupholder I sent you?"

"Oh, thanks for that," said Dru. "It works great—he hasn't asked me to hold his coffee once since it arrived."

"One is happy to be of service," said Wheelbarrowx.

Regina looked back and forth between Leery and Dru for a moment. "I'm betting you didn't call us down here for a reunion. What's up?"

Leery took a sip of coffee. "You didn't hear this from us." He glanced around. "It looks like there's a serial killer dropping vampires in Central Park."

"Bugger me dead!" said Bryant. "How many?"

"We don't know yet," said Dru. "I think we're up to five. Staked and buried head down."

"Paladins," muttered Bryant. "That's their trick."

"I don't think so," said Dru. "Is there even an active guild hall in New York City?"

"Your boss should know," said Regina.

"She's not a paladin," said Leery. "That was her father. Epatha Van Helsing is one hundred percent cop."

"Fair suck of the sav!" muttered Bryant. "Apples fall down, sepo."

"Yeah? How alike are you and your father?"

"Fair point." Bryant tossed his head. "But still something to look into. I'll ask back at the office."

"Right," said Leery. "But keep this under your hat for now. There's going to be a task force, of course, and I'll push the lieu to request you two."

"Meanwhile, we'll feel around about the MO. Anything else you can give us?" asked Regina.

"Not yet. Our ME is examining the bodies as we find them. She may turn something up."

"If we have the ME send you copies, is there any chance you can run pictures of the vics through that fancy magic box that matches pictures to names?" asked Leery.

"You mean our facial recognition software?"

"Or that," said Leery with a nod.

"We do have the identity of one of the victims," said Dru. "Antoine LaSalle. They may be related somehow."

Wheelbarrowx laughed and shook his head. "Kismet finally caught up to that jack bastard, eh?"

"Seems that way," said Dru. "You were embedded with the Dead Set for months, right?"

Regina nodded.

"We wondered about the possibility of the Set taking LaSalle out as punishment," said Leery.

"Could be," said Bryant.

Leery nodded. "That's what I thought. The others..."

Regina shrugged. "No telling how long those stiffs have been planted, right? At least not until your ME checks them out."

"Right."

"Maybe you found the Dead Set's dumping ground. It's convenient if nothing else."

"Where do we start?" asked Dru. "Who do we go see?"

Bryant turned his gaze on Dru. "Maybe your father can help."

Dru grimaced. "He's not affiliated with the Dead Set."

Regina crossed her arms and looked at the toes of her boots. "No, but he knows people who are."

"My father knows lots of vampires."

"Exactly our point," said Bryant. "He's old. His position in Gehenna puts him near the top of the pecking order." Bryant shrugged. "He knows people, and people turn to him for favors, for introductions. He might know someone with the pull to off LaSalle."

"Who else?" asked Leery.

Bryant and Regina exchanged a glance. "Marlow?" said Regina after a moment. "He probably took over for LaSalle."

"The guy who proved himself able to disappear so good that neither the NYPD nor the CBI can find him? Great."

"Oh, I bet we can find him," said Regina.

"Now that we're properly motivated," added Bryant.

4

After saying their farewells, Leery and Dru sat in the car as the pink Cube backed into traffic and pulled away. Leery reached for his last *trenta* and took a sip. "We can try to track down Marlow on our own if you want."

"No, they're right. Daddy's the best bet." Dru rolled down her window. "Gregory?"

With a crackling sound like that of a power transformer, Gregory appeared beside the car, bent at the waist. "Princess?"

"Could you ask Daddy to come here? We need to speak to him about a case."

"Certainly, Princess." Gregory's gaze flicked to Leery's, and he gave a solemn nod. "Detective."

"Hiya, Gregory."

"One moment."

Dru nodded, and the demon disappeared. A moment later, the armored SUV screeched to a halt next to them. Gregory got out and walked toward the Crown Vic.

Leery rolled down the window. "You should do Diner Drop, Gregory."

"I should do what?"

Dru shook her head.

"Dinner Delivery. Food Fling. Grub Grab." He flapped his hand. "What do I mean, Dru?"

She sighed, but her eyes twinkled. "Why don't you Giggle it?"

"Giggle?" His momentary look of confusion melted into a lopsided grin. "Oh, I get it. Cute, Dru-baby. Cute."

"Yes, I am." She leaned forward. "Don't mind us, Gregory."

The lava demon nodded once, his orange-glowing gaze snapping from Leery to Dru. "As you say, Princess." He continued to her door and opened it. "Your father awaits in the SUV."

They got out and climbed into the back of the brutish-looking vehicle. Hercule greeted them with a smile and a nod. "*Bonjour, ma chérie,*" he said, taking Dru's hand. "And to you, my friend." He nodded at Leery.

"*Tiens,* Hercule."

"How is your lovely daughter?"

"Busy with her own life," Leery said with a sad smile.

"Yes. This is the way of daughters." Hercule glanced at Dru and smiled to soften his words. "It is a father's place to stand back and be there when they call."

"Daddy, we caught a big case this morning." A pensive expression settled on Dru's features. "We found a vampire staked and buried head down."

"*C'est épouvantable!* Do I know this vampire?"

Dru pursed her lips, and a line appeared between her brows.

"It's Antoine LaSalle," said Leery.

"He said you knew one another during the War," said Dru.

Hercule's gaze drifted from Leery's to hers. "*Oui.* I knew *le vieux glos pautonnier.*" His face settled into a frown of distaste.

"Uh, my high school French—"

"Old gluttonous evildoer," said Hercule. "He descends from an unfaithful and wicked line. We fought against a common enemy"—he glanced at Leery and bowed his head—"if you will pardon the expression. I worked with him when circumstances demanded it, but I never cared for his...*comment le dis tu*...school of thought."

"Ah. He mentioned you had drifted apart."

"*Non*," said the old vampire. "My daughter, it is more correct to say we were never anything other than apart. We had no friendship, nothing beyond the work." He shook his head emphatically. "No, Antoine LaSalle and I were not friends, but I did know him."

"What about other Dead Setters?" asked Leery.

Hercule shrugged. "I know many people, many *vampires*, Leery. Some of my acquaintances are involved with that organization on a social level but no deeper—or so they tell me. I'm sure at least a few have a deeper involvement."

"What about Marlow, Daddy?"

Hercule nodded. "*Oui.* At one time, I associated with a vampire named Marlow."

"Were you friends?"

"Of a fashion," he said with a twitch of his shoulders. "Things were different back then, *mon amour.* Times were...darker. The Covenancy did not yet exist, and we supernatural beings were left to determine our own path, to solve our own problems."

"Marlow was a problem, then?"

Hercule's eyebrows rose, and the corners of his mouth turned downward. "I wouldn't say that, exactly. But vampires tended not to congregate often. We had traditions...each of us had territorial rights for"—he glanced at Leery—"the purposes of feeding, for instance."

"And Marlow didn't respect those traditions?" asked Leery.

"Not as such." Hercule flapped a hand. "He pushed things, stepped across lines when he thought he could get away with it."

"I see."

"Daddy, do you have any idea where he is?"

"No, *ma fille.* I haven't spoken with him in...oh, say four or five centuries."

"Not since you married Mother, then?"

Hercule nodded. "She doesn't like him."

"Then can you give us the list of vampires associated with the Dead Set?" asked Leery.

"*Assurément.* I know of a handful who are here in Manhattan. Étienne Rousseau, Nokomis Spencer, Leonid Polidori, and Judith Parish, to name those I recall off the top of my head."

"Any ideas who might be more involved than the others?"

Hercule pursed his lips and scratched his head. "Were I to guess, Nokomis Spencer and Leonid Polidori. The latter finds his status in life troublesome, coming from the peasant class as he does. And Nokomis…well, she is a handful no matter what she's doing." He frowned. "I'm sorry I cannot provide better guidance on the matter. I've always thought the Dead Set philosophy would fade over time. Perhaps I need to pay more attention to it."

"I don't know about that, Hercule. They were on the CBI's radar not too long ago. Usually, that means groups like the Set don't have long to live," said Leery. "Besides, you've given us a place to start."

"I will ask around to see if anyone knows Marlow's location."

"Thanks, Daddy," said Dru.

5

They waved as Gregory started the demonic engine of the SUV and shrieked away, then turned and got back into their cruiser. Dru started the car and pulled out into traffic. Her phone rang, and she glanced at Leery. "Grab that for me, will you?"

Leery picked up her phone, answered it, and switched to speakerphone without any trouble—a fact which evoked a sly smile from Dru. "Hello?" she said.

"Dru? Liz Hendrix."

"Hiya, Liz. Leery here. Before you get started, Dru's driving and can't hit me."

"Well, that's too bad. Maybe she can keep count and hit you when she stops? Let this be number one."

Dru chuckled. "I can do that."

"Good. I found something."

"What's that?" asked Leery.

"Cinnamon and cloves."

"What?"

"You heard me. Your killer treated the bodies with a concoction of cinnamon and cloves. They reek of it."

Dru stole a quick glance at Leery. "What about other scents?"

"Like what?"

"Animals," said Leery. "Mulled wine."

"Were they killed at a Yule party?" Liz asked with a chuckle. "All you're missing is frankincense and spruce."

"Um."

"Come on, Oriscoe. You can't tell me you've never paid attention to that big nose of yours at holiday parties."

"Well..."

"Men," said Liz. "I didn't detect anything but the two spices. Which isn't to say no other scents existed—these remains were bagged and transported through the city streets, then stored in the ME vaults with all the associated odors." She cleared her throat. "What's this about?"

"We went to LaSalle's house," said Leery. "It reeked of cinnamon, cloves, mulled wine, and wild animals."

"I'll send word to my techs," said Liz. "I'll instruct them to make an olfactory analysis before the corpses are exhumed."

"What's the count so far?" asked Leery.

"Well, you furry bastard, counting the one rolling in as we speak, that brings us to six."

"This is going to be a long day."

Liz grunted. "Dru?"

"Yes, Liz?"

"Add another."

Dru laughed. "Will do."

6

Nokomis Spencer and Leonid Polidori both lived on the Upper East Side, though the former lived in a five-story walk-up off East 85th Street, and the latter owned an entire building on the corner of Fifth Avenue and East 75th Street. There was an annoying wrought iron fence taking up half the sidewalk around Spencer's building, so Dru had to park in the crosswalk.

Leery craned his neck to look up at the building, then whistled. "I bet the rent in this place is more than what I pay."

"Living on the sidewalk behind this building costs more than you pay."

He shrugged his shoulders. "Ah, but then you'd miss the ambience."

"Right."

"What's a place like this go for?"

"On Fifth Avenue? Call it twenty million to buy it."

Leery whistled again.

"Why, are you thinking of moving?"

"Sure. I just need to save my entire salary for about two hundred years first."

"It would do you good to get out of that crackerbox."

"Hey, I like the place. The smell of old socks, the closet-sized kitchen, the balcony that looks out onto an alley. What could be better?"

"A roommate?" Dru grinned.

"Uh... You mean like Gonofrio?"

"Relax. It was a joke."

"I knew that," said Leery. "I was joking, too."

They went inside and stopped at the desk. "We're here to see Nokomis Spencer," said Leery.

The wight in the doorman's uniform behind the desk gave him the once over, then arched one eyebrow. "Will she know what this is about?" he grated in a voice that sounded like stone grinding on stone.

"God, I hope not," said Leery, then he flipped his badge on the counter. "And you'd better not give her a hint."

"I have to tell her *something*," he said with a sniff.

"Tell her Princess Drusilla bat Agrat is here," said Dru. "Tell her Hercule DuSang sends his greetings."

The wight squinted his clouded eyes at Dru. "Princess who?"

"Drusilla bat Agrat of Gehenna, daughter of Hercule DuSang and Agrat bat Mahlat. Niece of His Majesty, Lucifer ben Mahlat." Leery grinned at him. "You don't get out much, do you?"

"I have to work." The wight grimaced and reached for the phone. He punched in a number. "Mistress, there is a woman at the desk. She says she is Princess Drusilla bat Agrat—" The wight looked her up and down. "Yes, Mistress. Dark hair, red eyes, curved horns emerging from the top of her forehead." He listened for a moment, then nodded. "Of course, Mistress." He hung up the phone.

"Mistress Spencer will see you. Take the elevator to the thirteenth floor."

"See? That wasn't so hard," said Leery. "Hey, you know they have these tanning parlors now. Might do wonders for that complexion."

The wight sneered at him and turned his face away.

The elevator doors opened on the granite-tiled opulence of the penthouse. "I bet this place costs more than twenty million," whispered Leery.

"Five times that, were I inclined to sell," said a cultured voice from the room to their left. "Come in, Your Grace."

Leery and Dru walked into a huge sitting room furnished in chrome and black leather. An olive-skinned woman, who appeared less than thirty years old, sat in a leather sling-chair, one leg crossed over the other, red-soled Louboutin leopard skin pumps on her feet. She wore a peach silk dress and lots of gold jewelry. As Dru entered, she slowly stood and bowed her head. "Your Grace, I am Nokomis Spencer."

"*Enchantée*," said Dru. "This is Leery Oriscoe."

Nokomis's gaze flitted toward Leery without seeing him and returned to Dru's face. "It's true, then," she said in a dull voice.

"What is?" asked Leery.

Nokomis didn't react and only continued to look at Dru.

"What is?" asked Dru.

"That your father has abandoned certain..." Again, her gaze flicked toward Leery. "Certain long-standing traditions, shall we say?"

Dru's laugh sprinkled the air. "Oh, yes. Daddy has renounced his vile bigotry toward the wolves."

Though Nokomis tried to conceal it, her upper lip trembled with her desire to sneer.

"But we're not here to speak of such things," said Dru. "Daddy said you're the type of vampire who'd be swayed by the nonsense espoused by the Dead Set."

Silence fell around them as Nokomis narrowed her eyes and frowned. "That's offensive, Princess."

Dru shrugged. "So are the philosophies of the Set—the *real* Dead Set, anyway."

"If insulting me is the only thing you—"

"Antoine LaSalle is dead," said Leery. "Staked and buried head down."

Nokomis turned her head slowly to face Leery. "What did you say?"

"You heard me. Someone used a runed stake to give him true-death, then buried him in Central Park with his feet pointing at the sky. Maybe you know something about that?"

She shook her head, a glimmer of red welling up in the corners of her eyes. "LaSalle is just…"

"No," said Dru. "He's gone. The true-death, as my partner said. He won't be back."

"I…" Nokomis squeezed her eyes shut and covered her lips with shaking fingers. "That's not possible."

"Believe me," said Leery, "it is."

"No one in the Dead Set would dream of crossing LaSalle, let alone…"

"Maybe it's retaliation for drawing all that media attention at the end of the summer," said Dru. "Punishment for letting things get out of hand."

"Who is in charge of your little clique?" asked Leery. "Who was LaSalle's boss?"

Nokomis opened her eyes a sliver's worth. "I can't say."

"You don't know, or you can't say?"

She shook her head and clenched her jaw.

"Look, Nokomis," said Dru. "You know who I am. You know who my father is. Do you really think either one of us would threaten vampirekind?"

Spencer scoffed, then dabbed at the corners of her eyes with her fingers. They came away bloody, which seemed to irritate her even more. "You and your father can burn in the sunlight for eternity as far as I'm concerned!" she snapped. "Now, I want both of you to get out of my house. Get out of my *building*! And don't come back."

"Listen, Spencer—"

"No, *wolf*. You listen to me. If you don't have a warrant to search my flat, get out. If you want to question me, submit your questions to my magister, and if I feel like it, I will answer. If you want to bring me in, get an arrest warrant!"

"And your magister is?" asked Dru in a mild tone.

"Jeffery DeRothenberg. Now, get out!"

"I should have guessed," said Leery. "One bloodless fool representing another."

"*Get out!*" Nokomis shouted, springing to her feet and pointing at the elevator.

"Relax," said Dru. "We'll go."

"You'd think you'd want to help us," said Leery as he walked toward the elevator. "Especially since the news of LaSalle's death made you cry."

Nokomis whirled around, shunning them with her back, her silence, her impotent fury.

7

Leonid Polidori also lived on the top floor of a building, though it was hardly a penthouse. After climbing five flights of stairs, sweat trickled down Leery's face and neck, and he felt a little winded. "Couldn't...have...an..." he gasped.

"Elevator," finished Dru. "It'll do you good."

"What...happened...to...me...taking...it..."

"Easy? I let you rest on each floor, didn't I?"

Leery rolled his eyes and leaned against the wall at the top of the stairs. "How about...one of those...invigoration rune sets?"

Dru pursed her lips and shook her head. "You don't need them anymore. You need to get your legs back, that's all."

"Funny...this feels more...like my lungs...have fallen out."

Dru chuckled, low and throaty. "Them, too. We'll get you back to fighting fit in no time, Leery. You'll see." She cocked her head to the side. "Though you never did like climbing stairs."

"Hey, why would there be elevators...if stairs are so good for you?"

"For lazy werewolves, Leery."

"I'm not lazy, I'm..." He squinted up at the ceiling, his lips moving. Finally, he shrugged. "I'm not lazy, I'm *discerning* about how I get my exercise. And trust me, Dru, there are far better ways than climbing stairs."

"Healthier or more fun?" She bent her head forward and let her hair cascade over her shoulders, then peeked at him through the curtain of sable.

"There's a difference? But for future conversation, let's just say I come down on the side of more fun." She grinned at him—that *special* grin—and all of a sudden, he felt like panting again. "So...uh..." he croaked. "What apartment is Polidori's?"

Dru's eyes sparkled for a moment. "You always know the right thing to say to make a girl feel special."

"Yeah. It's a gift." He grinned *his* special grin right back at her, and she laughed aloud.

"Come on," she said. "It's this way."

She led him to the door marked 5J and pointed at it. Leery made a fist and pounded on the door. "Leonid Polidori!" he called. "You home, Leo?"

The ambient sounds that had flowed around them since they'd stepped out of the stairwell vanished, leaving a crypt-like silence in their wake.

Leery pounded on the door again. "Come on, Polidori! Your neighbors don't like us standing in the hall."

The locks rattled on 5J's door, then it opened a crack. "What?"

"Detective Oriscoe, Supernatural Inquisitors Squad. I've got questions for you, Leo."

"*Leonid,* if you please. And what questions?"

Leery made a show of looking down the hall. "Your house or mine, Leonid."

"Fine, fine." Leonid closed the door, and the chain rattled. The door opened a little, then stopped.

Leery pushed the door the rest of the way open, then stepped inside and followed Leonid down the short, crowded hallway. The apartment stank of decay and decomposition. The cream-colored paint on the walls had cracked and peeled in places, dust coated every available surface, and stacks of newspapers lined the walls.

"Excuse the mess," said Leonid with an uneven grin. "The maid has the century off." The old vampire sank into a recliner so worn it appeared to be custom fit for his body. "Shove that crap onto the floor," he said, pointing at an old couch from the 1970s. "Make yourselves at home."

He glanced at Dru, and his left eye widened a skosh. Then his nostrils flared, and his gaze snapped to Leery's. "Pack? You *dare*—"

"The war's over, pal," said Leery. "Hundreds of years before I was even born. And I'm a cop, so stow that crap."

"My partner forgot to introduce me," said Dru. "I'm Drusilla bat Agrat. Hercule DuSang is my father."

Leonid turned a wide-eyed gaze on her. "You don't look like a princess."

"She cleans up nice," said Leery. "Antoine LaSalle is dead."

"Well, of *course,* he's dead! He's a *vampire.*"

"Not undead, Polidori. Dead-dead. As in staked and buried with his soles to the sky."

Leonid pursed his lips and glanced at Dru. When she nodded, his brows bunched. "Well, that's the first bit of good news I've had since...well, let's just say it's been *centuries.* Who did it? I owe them a thank-you note."

"We were hoping you could help us with that," said Leery.

Leonid grinned, exposing his fangs. "Incompetence is not something I can fix."

"Yeah, keep that sort of thing up," said Leery. "I mean, it's not like you didn't make yourself a suspect with that reaction."

Polidori threw back his head and laughed. "Me? You suspect me of killing LaSalle?" He laughed long and hard, and when his mirth was exhausted, he wound down to a few chuckles and a wide grin. "If I could have done the deed, LaSalle wouldn't have made it through the 1700s. The man was a cretin, but he had *power,* wolf. Real power."

"Because of the Dead Set?"

Leonid chuckled again. "That? No. That was something to do in his *retirement,* wolf.

Antoine LaSalle was—" He bit off the sentence and squinted at Dru. "Tell Hercule I wouldn't speak of LaSalle's past."

"I'm sure my father doesn't care. He broke off contact with LaSalle at the end of the War of Fangs."

"Is that what he told you?" asked Leonid with eyes a-twinkle. "Then it must be true."

"Listen, Polidori, we're not here to dredge up old slights and ancient history. We're out to solve LaSalle's murder in the here and now."

Leonid shrugged and spread his hands.

"Our working theory is that the Dead Set had him killed to—" Leonid burst into laughter and Leery stopped talking, squinting down at the vampire.

Still laughing, Leonid waved his hands. "Sorry, sorry. It's the picture of one of those ineffectual young bloodsuckers going after LaSalle. Truly comedic."

"And Marlow?" asked Dru.

Leonid sobered and sniffed. "That is another matter. But think of it like this: Marlow and LaSalle have known one another since the early 1400s. Both knew the other's capabilities and proclivities. They have maintained an association since the War of Fangs. What would possibly drive Marlow to banish LaSalle now?"

"We understand that Marlow viewed the traditions of your kind with a certain disdain."

Leonid shrugged. "That is well known, but he never disrespected anyone with the power to do him in. Never."

"Then who?"

Leonid gazed at the shade-covered window. "Someone from the outside."

"Outside of what? The Dead Set?"

"Well, surely the Set, but I mean outside of vampire society."

Leery grimaced and glanced at Dru.

"You mean the paladins?" she asked.

Leonid flapped his hand. "Maybe, but they always tended to avoid the strongest of our kind. Speak with your father about them."

"I'll ask it again," said Leery. "Then who?"

The vampire shook his head, a pensive expression twisting his features. "I'd say one of the lower caste, but they have no hope of dispatching even the weakest of my kind."

"You mean the zees?" asked Leery.

"Yes, of course."

"What if they acted in concert? If they banded together—"

"No, you don't understand," said Leonid. "One like LaSalle can command obedience. Certain words in the right language. Certain runes, invocations." Leonid sniffed. "We, sir, are masters of the undead."

Leery lifted his hands out to his side. "Then who?"

"A group of vampires might do it, but LaSalle would not go down without a fight. There would be injuries."

"The Nephilim?" asked Dru.

"They can't be bothered with us. The Angelic Host as well." He played with his lip a moment. "And the manner of the burial. This smacks of age-old wisdom and practices."

"So we've circled back to Marlow."

"Not necessarily," said Leonid. "But perhaps someone like him. Hercule, for instance."

"I think we can leave him out of this," said Leery.

Leonid's face split with a nasty smile. "If you'd known him in the War, you would not exclude him so easily." He turned to Dru. "It could also be your royal mother. She...*disapproved* of LaSalle."

"All that might be true," said Leery, "but why wait? Her Royal Highness could have dispatched LaSalle at any time."

Leonid lifted one shoulder and let it drop. "Who knows the myriad ways of Gehenna?"

"I do," said Dru firmly. "Where is Marlow?"

Leonid inclined his head and peeked at her from under his bushy brows. "Are you sure you want to find him?"

"Stop playing games, Polidori, or I'll run you in."

The vampire chuckled. "Look around, wolf. Do you suppose I wouldn't welcome such excitement?" He leaned back in the recliner and put his feet up with a clunk of the chair's mechanism. "No, Detective. I don't think Marlow is your killer. I don't think the Dead Set had anything to do with this. I think someone has decided to settle an old score. You should be looking at LaSalle's past, at his enemies, not his friends."

"And what about you, Leonid? Were you his friend or his enemy?"

"Me? I'm too insignificant to befriend, or even notice, and far too weak to rate enmity. The powerful have ignored me for centuries, Detective. I'm no threat to anyone."

Leery sniffed. "What's that smell?"

Leonid waved a languid hand over his shoulder. "Blood. Old blood."

"From?"

"I buy from the Manhattan blood bank like all others of my kind who can't maintain a hunting license."

"And I suppose you have receipts?"

Leonid lifted an eyebrow. "Somewhere." He waved his hand at the messy apartment. "You're welcome to look."

"What can you tell us about Étienne Rousseau and Judith Parish?"

Polidori shook his head. "I don't know them. I've heard their names at parties, but I couldn't pick them out of a crowd."

Leery looked him up and down. "I've been to one of the Dead Set parties. How do you warrant an invitation to such a froufrou soiree?"

"Invitation?" Leonid laughed. "I *work* at those parties, Detective. I *serve* those froufrou guests. I decant blood, I keep it warmed, and I walk around with a tray of glasses full of it."

"And Nokomis Spencer?" asked Dru.

"That old bitch? I know her. What of it?"

"Could she have had something to do with LaSalle's murder?"

Polidori snorted. "She loved the old bastard. Can you imagine? She *loved* him!" He burst into another round of laughter. "As though LaSalle would even notice, let alone care for anyone, beneath his station. She's a fool."

Dru looked at Leery and arched an eyebrow.

Leery sighed. "All right, Polidori. That's all we have for now. Don't leave town."

Again, Leonid laughed. "And leave all this?" He lifted his hands out to his sides and smirked.

8

The Crown Vic rocked as Leery settled into the passenger seat. He reached for the last *trenta,* picked it up, shook it, and frowned. "Have you been drinking my coffee?"

Dru chuckled. "Without sugar? Not on your life."

Leery sniffed and put the empty cup back in the cupholder. "Let's find a Starbucks and figure out what to do—"

His phone jangled, and he seemed to answer the call by accident. "Hello?"

"Oriscoe? Van Helsing."

"Hiya, Lieu. What's up?"

"We made a discovery down here in the North Woods."

"More bodies?"

The was a long pause, then Van Helsing said, "You could say that. As they exhumed one of the vampires, the ME crew spotted a bunch of matted hair in the walls of the pit. They uncovered the top of a head, and further investigation revealed a mass grave."

"A mass grave? In Central Park?"

"You heard me, Oriscoe. Eight bodies stacked up like cord wood."

"The killer abandoned the head-down orientation?"

"These aren't vampires, Leery."

"No?"

"Elves. Dark elves, wood elves, high elves— the only thing they have in common is almond-shaped eyes and pointy ears."

"But—"

"We're bringing in the Ceebies. I've requested their ground-penetrating radar, in addition to a cadre of corpse-dogs."

"What's going on here, Lieu?"

"Damfino. Aren't you supposed to be telling me? You and your bang up to the elephant bit o' raspberry quit killing the canary and find me some answers."

"We're on it, Lieu, but to tell you the truth, we're not having much success. We're looking into the Dead Set because of LaSalle."

"I think that's a good angle," said Epatha. "That and the paladins. Though neither group gives one rat's ass about elves."

"Vampires and elves…" murmured Leery. "What's the connection, Lieu?"

"It's a carriwitchett, to be sure. It would help if we knew who any of them were."

"And how they connected with LaSalle."

"Maybe there isn't any connection. Maybe this is all…"

"Random," said Leery. "Lieu… It's time we start calling this what it is."

"No, Oriscoe. Not yet."

"But, Epatha, these victims show every appearance of being selected at random. And no one can deny the pattern—at least as far as the dumping grounds go."

"You might be right, Leery, but keep it under your hat. Think about what will happen if we make that call."

"Hey, Lieu, I don't care about the credit if we can stop—"

"Not yet, Oriscoe, and it's not about credit or stats. I have a feeling about this, is all. It's not what it appears."

Leery said nothing for a few moments, letting that sink in. "Well, your gut is legendary, Lieu."

"Did you just call me fat, Oriscoe?"

9

Outside the ME's office, Leery and Dru waited in the car, sipping coffee. Vinny Gonofrio and Kathandra Earbes were on their way up from 1PP, making a special trip so Gonofrio could examine the runes carved into the stakes with his own eyes and special senses.

"So, Leery," said Dru.

"So, Dru."

"Are you planning on spending the night in your skivvies, belching and enjoying being alone?"

"I don't know about all that," said Leery, turning to look out the side window. "I've lived alone a long time, but I'll tell you, a guy could get used to the lap of luxury I've spent the past few months in."

"Not to mention having the attention of the Prince of Darkness."

"It's true that Luci and I have had a chance to—"

"Will you miss it? The camaraderie?"

"Well, sure. Your uncle's a consummate host. I'll miss *him*."

"And..." Dru dropped her gaze to her lap, where she found her hands trying to kill each other and made them stop. "Is..."

"Is Luci the only one I'll miss? No."

Dru lifted her head and peeked at him.

"I mean, there's Angie, too." He grinned wolfishly.

With a chuckle, she punched him in the shoulder.

"You're getting to like that part a little too much," he said. He gazed at her for a moment. His face grew solemn, and he opened his mouth, but before he could say more, Gonofrio and Earbes pulled up behind them and blipped the horn. "Oh, look, the kids are here," he said instead of whatever he'd almost said.

Dru frowned at her mirror. "Perfect timing," she muttered as Leery opened his door and got out.

"Hey, Kathandra. Vinny," Leery called. "Thanks for making the drive."

"No sweat," said Vinny. He reached into the backseat and pulled out a thermos, which he tossed to Leery. "Made with holy water, of course."

"If I didn't know better, Gonofrio, I'd swear you were an angel."

"Eh," said Vinny with a shrug. "I'm the best of both worlds."

Grinning, Leery spun the lid off and took a swig, then refilled his Starbucks cup and set the thermos in their car.

Dru stepped out of their cruiser and smiled at Earbes and Gonofrio. "Hey, Vinny. We've got a puzzle for you, so get your big brain all warmed up and ready."

"You mean with the runes?"

"More," said Leery, "but let's figure that part out first. Both Hendrix and Dru agree they are a mix of Enochian and something else. Something neither of them recognize, let alone can identify."

Vinny shrugged. "Simple enough."

The four went inside the building and took the elevator to Liz's floor. She was still in court, but her new assistant pulled LaSalle's remains from the coolers and arranged him on one of the metal tables.

Vinny approached the table, turning his head this way and then the other, then bending to the side, putting his head parallel to the floor. "Yep, that's Enochian," he said. "Oh, I see why she's having trouble with the rest. These are Proto-Elamite." He straightened up and shook his hand near his waist. "Calling it rare is like calling Dru pretty."

"Thank you," said Dru with a grin.

"But you can read it?"

"Omnilingual, remember?" said Vinny in an absent tone. He leaned over again, then whistled. "Gee, whoever inscribed these really didn't want this guy to come back."

"What's it say? Liz suspected the enchantments have something to do with dissipating the lifeforce of the thing staked."

"Hear ye," Vinny intoned. "And be ye forewarned, as this creature is dead, and should remain dead for— Well, there it enters the flesh." He walked around the table, his head still bent to the side. "Ah. Here's more.

Hear ye and be ye forewarned, as this foul creature traded his living soul for an abominable life in the shadows. He isn't using it, so—" He shook his head, then straightened and grabbed the stake. He heaved but only accomplished lifting LaSalle's torso from the table. "No, that won't do," he murmured. He moved around to stand at the head of the stainless-steel table, then narrowed his eyes and squinted at the tiny runes inscribed on the stake. "Ah. I see how to do it." He straightened and glanced at Dru. "You may want to step into the hall for a moment."

"No," she said. "I'm fine."

"I'm going to invoke..."

"Ah," she said. She backed to the doors and nodded. "That should do it."

Vinny looked as though he might want to argue, then nodded. "Suit yourself." He closed his eyes and tilted his head back. He raised his hands above his head like a revival tent preacher, then froze in that pose for a few breaths. When he spoke, his voice rolled forth like thunder across the plains, and Leery had the sense that everyone—*everything*—stopped to listen. He chanted, sounding every bit the Gregorian monk, and as the chant progressed, the stake first jiggled in its fleshly sheath, then wriggled, then began to hop up and down. Without opening his eyes, Vinny leaned forward and took the stake in his left hand, his right still held heavenward. His chant grew toward a crescendo, and the knuckles of his left hand blanched. As he uttered the last syllable, he wrapped his right hand around his left and jerked the stake from LaSalle's withered flesh.

"That was one helluva show, Vinny," said Leery. "Isn't that right, Dru?" He turned to where she'd stood a moment before, a smile plastered on his lips, but she was gone, only the subtle swinging of the door to mark her passage.

"Don't blaspheme, Leery," murmured Vinny. "Not with me."

"Sorry. No offense meant. Is it..." He pointed at the door.

"What?" asked Vinny. "Oh, yeah. I'm done."

"I'll go," said Kathandra, as she swept through the other door and beckoned.

Vinny set the stake on LaSalle's chest. "That took more than I thought it would," he said. "Whoever caused this stake to impale itself in this old vampire had more than a little bit of knowledge on his side. And raw magic."

"Yeah, we heard LaSalle was a font of hidden powers. That it would take someone like you describe to kill him."

Vinny squinted down at the stake. "Hear ye and be ye forewarned as, blah-blah-blah...here we go...should remain dead for his sins are great. Let no one resurrect this foul creature, let no one give him respite." He reached out and flipped the stake to its other side. "And this one: blah-blah-blah be forewarned blah-blah... He isn't using it so, let the lifeforce allotted to him be recast, sent into the void but called back to serve me, to nestle within the roots of my own life, to lend me its power, its vitality, its *life*." Vinny straightened and looked at Leery. "And there you go. Your perp is a lich."

"Crap," said Leery. "I hate those guys."

"Yeah, I can understand that," said Kathandra. "Always trying to take what doesn't belong to them. At least with a vampire, you know how he's going to come at you."

They fell silent and stared down at LaSalle's body. The color of his skin and hair leeched away to a faded gray. His body sagged toward the middle, then cracks zig-zagged through his skin, widening almost as fast as they lengthened. His fingers and toes crumbled first, too-long snakes of ash from a cigar left smoldering. His hands dwindled next, collapsing inward like empty husks of dry dirt. His disintegration progressed quickly, his bones and flesh decaying to nothing more than a pile of loose ash as they watched.

"I guess that's that," said Kathandra.

"The stake was the only thing keeping him around," said Vinny with a shrug. "When I pulled it, the clock started ticking. But something's bothering me about all this."

"You mean the fact that I left the thermos down in the car?" asked Leery, staring mournfully down into his cup.

"Why focus exclusively on vampires?" murmured Gonofrio.

"Yeah, uh, remember that 'more' we mentioned outside?"

Vinny arched an eyebrow.

"Vampires and elves."

"*Elves?*" asked Vinny.

Leery nodded. "That's what I said. I gotta say, Vinny, I hope that rings a bell with you because I have no ideas at all."

Vinny glanced at Earbes and shook his head. "I'll think on it."

"Anything else of interest on the stake itself?" asked Dru.

Vinny's eyes lit up. "Yeah. I've read the two parts that have to do with stealing lifeforce, but the other two sides are all about enchanting the stake itself. That's why I had to call on...why I had to do the chant. The stake says the wood is yew, carved from the 'living heart' of the 'Tree of Death' and prepared in the 'old way.' There's nature magic woven through the tight grain of the wood with death magic running counter-grain."

"Wow. That's a lot of overkill to take out someone like LaSalle."

Vinny nodded. "There's more to it. Themes of sacrifice and rebirth, resurrection of the dead, longevity—it's kind of a muddle. But"—he held up his index finger—"it's signed."

"Signed?"

"Yes. Right down here by the tip. It says, 'These things, I, Yoltomta, command.'"

"Somehow, I don't think that name will be in our databases."

"Probably not," said Vinny. "But it is a portmanteau of two Old Norse words. 'Yol,' which means 'Christmas,' and 'tomta', which means something akin to 'house elf.'"

"Wait a minute. You're not saying—"

"I'm just telling you what this says. It's signed by someone calling himself 'Christmas Elf.'"

"Great. A lunatic who's a lunatic."

"Nah," said Vinny. "A serial killer who's a lunatic."

"You know..." said Kathandra. "Maybe it's not a portmanteau, Vinny."

"No, Kath, it *is*—"

"Hear me out, Vinny. I have no doubt in your translation, but maybe it's a proper name. You know, like Smith or Baker."

"Christmaself?" asked Leery.

"Yes, but it's in Old Norse, right?"

"I see where you're going with this," said Vinny, grinning ear to ear. "And I think you might be onto something for once."

"Well, thanks a lot, Vinny," said Kathandra, staring daggers at him.

"Hey, you know I didn't mean it like that," he said. "You know how my mouth gets when I'm all excited. Sorry, okay? I'm sorry."

Earbes rolled her eyes heavenward and shook her head. "You're lucky I'm hard to offend, you big jackass."

"I am," said Vinny. "I need a library."

"How about Gerbil?" said Leery.

"Gerbil? I don't—"

Shaking her head, Dru said, "Google, Vinny. He means Google."

"Gerbil?" Vinny said with a laugh in his voice and a wide grin on his face. "Where'd you get that from, Leery?"

"Oh, you know. A pet store."

"You're really a lunatic, Oriscoe. You know that?" He cocked his head at Dru. "I mean, he knows that, right?"

Dru showed him a lopsided smile. "He knows. He thinks it's cute."

Vinny looked at Leery with a half-grin on his face. "Gerbil," he said and chuckled. "Lunatic."

"Yeah, I get that a lot," said Leery with a matching expression. "But, hey, everyone remembers my name."

"Speaking of names," said Vinny. "What's that Barghest called?"

"I'm not sure," said Dru. "He may not have a name."

"All dogs need names! You think Greek mythology would be the same with 'that three-headed dog' instead of Cerberus? Or Orthrus?"

"I can check for you," said Dru.

"Yeah, and can you find out how he's doing?"

"Yes, Leery already mentioned that."

"Oh, okay. Great. Thanks. Call me anytime."

"Well, Anytime, thanks for the coffee and reading the Proto-Eurythmics or whatever you called it," said Leery.

Vinny shook his head and looked at Dru. "All day, right? I mean, he never lets up?"

"Not for a second. He even joked when he looked like a marshmallow that had fallen into the fire."

"Life's too short to let a good joke go unsaid."

"Let me know when you come across one," said Dru in a droll voice.

Leery slapped his hand to his breast and pretended to stagger. "Hey, that hurts! This is the end..."

"You know werewolves are immortal, right?" asked Vinny. "He knows that, right?" he asked looking at Dru with a grin plastered on his face.

Dru only grinned back at him.

"Looks like we need the library after all," said Kathandra. "Google has nothing on Yoltomta, and if you type in Christmas elf, look out."

"Right," said Vinny. "I figured as much. Not just any old library will do. We need one with genealogical records."

Kathandra shrugged. "The New York Public Library has a division dedicated to genealogy."

"Then that's where we need to go." Vinny shrugged. "I've never been, so I can't speak to the quality of their records, but it's a start. We'll do that part, just get us tagged for the task force so Sherikins doesn't have another conniption fit."

10

Leery leaned forward and waved the thermos as Vinny and Kathandra pulled out into traffic and passed them. Vinny gave them a blip of the siren in answer. "He's not bad for one of the Nephilim. Definitely not what I expected," said Leery.

"Do you know other Nephilim?"

"Nah. Not really. But you expect them to be all holier-than-thou, all 'don't blaspheme, Leery,' crap like that."

"Vinny tells you that all the time."

"Yeah, but he doesn't *mean* it." He cocked his head. "Hey...you hear that?"

"Hear what, Leery?"

"Sounds like bells or something."

"What, like church bells?"

"Nah. Smaller than that."

"Cowbells?"

"Nah. Those little ones that people hang on their Christmas trees."

"Leery, we didn't—"

"How are you going to hear it if you're talking all the time? Listen for bells." He rolled down his window, eyes squinted up, head cocked. "They're getting closer."

Dru rolled down her window and stuck her head out. After a moment, she shook her head. "I need werewolf ears, I guess."

Leery opened the door and got out, peering first up, then down the street. "What *is* that?" he muttered. "Do you smell that?" he asked.

Dru got out and came around to stand next to him and sniffed the air. "Smell what?"

"Cinnamon."

"Do you still hear the bells?"

Leery nodded and then turned his face up to the sky. "Above us, now."

Dru began to draw gunmetal gray runes in the air. She linked the three runes with gray lines and set the whole thing spinning with a grunted spidery phrase. She flicked her fingers toward the sky, and the rotating rune set arced up toward the clouds. She drew a deep breath in through her nose. "Spicy. Cinnamon and cloves."

"Yeah," he said. "And musk."

"Musk?"

Leery nodded. "The animal smell from LaSalle's place. Like deer."

Dru frowned. "I'm not getting anything from the runes."

"I can't see anything, either." He turned in a circle. "The bells have stopped, but the scent is still there." He turned back toward the building. "It's coming from the roof of the building."

Dru nodded and chanted a phrase in the *Lingua Tenebris Lacuna.* "Let's go. I set my runes to hover over the building, but there's still nothing to see."

They ran up the steps and into the lobby, then pressed the button for the top floor. Leery paced in the small confines of the elevator car as it rose ponderously upward, and as soon as the door opened, he took an enormous sniff. "It's faded," he said, "but still here."

"The bodies!" Dru cried and mashed the button for Liz's floor.

Leery nodded and kicked off his shoes. He went to work on his belt and tie as Dru began a set of crimson runes that seemed to suck the air from the small car, blazing and flickering like raw, open flames. Leery swept his shirt and coat off over his head and dropped his trousers, kicking them after the shoes.

"What do you think it is?" asked Dru.

"Animal, judging by the musk. Magical or enchanted, no doubt."

"Enchanted by who?"

"Yoltomta," he grated as he began his change.

Dru added the last rune to her set and connected them in a nine-pointed star with lines the color of hot magma. She cocked back her hand as though to throw a ball, then stood staring at the elevator doors as fur sprouted across Leery's back and chest.

A growl began deep in his chest, rumbling like a tremor building toward a massive earthquake. The fur of his head knitted itself into a *yarmulke* tight against his lupine skull, and the charm Lucifer had gifted him with transformed into a black woolen hat. He flexed, and his muscles rippled with no sign of the massive injuries Dr. Agon had inflicted. His fur seemed glossy and thick, like that of a much younger wolf. He snarled at the doors as the elevator dinged, then crouched, his muscles bunching and twitching with the urge to run, to pounce, to attack.

The doors began to open onto the black satin of the darkened hallway, and somewhere lost in all that black, a woman screamed. Leery howled and grabbed the edges of the doors, forcing them apart with brute strength. He sprang into the darkness, a quivering snarl deforming his lips, showing his fangs to all and sundry.

Dru stepped out of the elevator car behind him, looking left, then right toward Liz's lab. Leery was nothing more than a dark lump against a black background, but he was moving toward the lab. With one last look behind her, Dru turned and followed.

Leery ran on all fours, his nose up in the air, the scent of cinnamon and cloves itching the back of his throat. His eyes watered with the power of the odor, and, unconsciously, he growled with irritation. He barged through the double doors that led to Hendrix's workroom, a howl slamming past his lips as he reared to his back legs and threw his arms wide.

The overhead fluorescents blinked and strobed, an insane light show from a hyperkinetic rave, light and dark usurping the room from one another every half-second or so. With his eyelids crammed together, Leery clawed the light switch, ending the orgy of blinding flashing. He opened his eyes and took in the room.

In the center of the room, an overturned exam table lay in a puddle of ash—the remains of Antoine LaSalle—and, next to it, the unconscious body of a lab tech, her blonde hair strewn in LaSalle's ashes. Along the far edge of the room, cooler doors hung open, lay smashed to the floor, or wobbled on one hinge. The spicy odor pervaded the room, overpowering even the scents of putrefaction, putrescence, and decay.

Behind him, Dru clattered up the hall toward the room, the heels of her four-thousand-dollar boots clattering on the linoleum tiles in the hall. Across the room, something shifted in the darkness, and Leery's gaze snapped to the sound. He inhaled through his lupine nose, filtering the scent, distilling it, searching for its source. He dropped into a ready stance and crept forward, his feet seeming to know where to go, what to avoid for maximum stealth.

Under the cinnamon and clove scent hung the bitter-clean smell of arctic expanses, of snow and ice in massive quantities. Underneath that wafted an earthy smell—like the interior of a deep cave or the basement of a barn. Not pleasant to his nose, but not unpleasant either. He padded on, walking almost exclusively on the pads of his toes, nerves taut, ready to pounce on his prey or to dive away from a bigger predator.

Out in the hall, Dru slid to a stop just beyond the double doors. She paused a moment to create a second rune set, this one glowing electric blue in the gloom, twenty-seven runes connected with a mess of crisscrossing golden lines. Controlling a rune set with either hand, she kicked the double doors open and jumped through them.

Leery didn't even pause when the doors slammed open. He'd smelled Dru in the hall and knew she must have been preparing her spells. But the thing he stalked started, sending things from Liz's worktable clattering and smashing to the floor.

Leery pounced, arms thrown wide, a silent snarl quivering on his lips, the scent of cinnamon clotting in his throat like old blood. He landed amid a sea of broken glass, of strewn papers, of the metal accoutrements of Liz's work, but with the grace of his wolfen cousins, his feet landed without injury on floor tiles clear of debris. A shadow bolted to the left as Leery landed, and he snatched at it, digging his fingers into long, gnarled hair. He tightened his hand into a fist, but with a savage jerk, his prey pulled away, leaving him with nothing but dry, brittle hair. He howled a warning to Dru and spun around, ears perked and bent forward.

Silence fell over the room as his howl faded, and no one moved. Dru stood in front of the doors to the hall, a crimson blaze in one hand, the cool blue rune set in the other. Shadows flickered in time with the crimson light.

"You are under arrest," Dru said into the silence. "You can't escape."

A child-like laugh rang out, and Leery snapped his head toward the corner between the lab counter and the rear wall. He was almost sure that was where the sound had originated. He crept toward it, stalking through the shadowy room, staring at the dark space hardly wide or tall enough to hide a five-year-old child.

Halfway there, he paused and turned his nose toward the door. The cinnamon smell had grown stronger. He glanced at the shadow-swathed corner, then back at the doors, and as he did, the laugh rang out again. He beckoned Dru with one hand and pointed at the doors with the other.

She stepped away from the doors, coming to where the foot of Liz's exam table had once stood, then turned to face the door. She lifted the flickering crimson rune set higher, and the laughter tickled the air for the third time.

Leery sprang, extending his arms over his head, stretching out his long, lean body. He dropped his feet at the last moment and sank into a crouch that blocked the murky corner, then thrust his hands into the darkness.

With another laugh, a short creature ran up the wall, footfalls thumping on the drywall. Leery lunged up at it, wrapping his long fingers around one ankle and jerking the creature back. The thing squawked as it fell into Leery's waiting grasp.

The doors hammered open and five short shapes barreled into the room. Dru hurled her crimson rune set at the floor in front of the door, and magenta fire erupted where it struck, shooting bands of fire to the left and the right, fencing off the room's only exit to the hall. The explosive combustion caught some of the small attackers midstride, and they shrieked as the flames overtook them. Their cries, however, lasted only a moment, cutting off in mid-scream as the creatures blinked away with a loud pop.

Leery wrapped his arms around the little creature he'd caught, hugging the thing to his chest. It reeked of both cinnamon and unclean animal pens the world over and felt like no more than a collection of sharp elbows and knees swaddled in unkempt hair. The thing twisted and struggled in his grasp without making a sound.

Near the door, Dru began another gray rune set, still holding the bright blue one high over her head, her gaze dancing toward the shadows, looking for the other invaders from the hall. She cast her new rune set, and brilliant blue-white light bathed the room. Under the rune set's harsh glare, she began another crimson set of runes.

Leery squinted down at the little creature thrashing in his arms, as much to protect his eyes from the bright light as to see what he held. Abruptly, the creature in Leery's grasp gave up, lying still against the werewolf's fur, breathing hard, but relaxed to the tips of his tiny fingers. The creature looked up at him, the picture of perfect calm, gaze resting on his easily. He was about thirty-five inches tall, covered in matted gray hair, with a bulbous nose and large round eyes. Tiny horns grew from his hairline over the outside edges of his almond-shaped eyes. His clothing was dark, matte-blacks and dark grays, and on his hand-like feet, he wore nothing at all. Leery's ears perked at the sound of tiny feet pounding across the room. He whirled around, his gaze ripped from the small creature in his arms and darting from one dark spot to the next across the room.

Dru hurried the crimson rune set, snapping lines between her runes and pounding out the words in the *Verba Patiendi*. "Leery, look out!" she cried.

Leery started and looked around him, but nothing moved. Too late, he remembered the creature in his arms had been *running straight up the wall.* He lifted his gaze to the ceiling in time to see three exact replicas leering down at him.

Then they pounced, tiny fangs bared, tiny hands curled into fists. They dropped on him from above like Lilliputian paratroopers. Elbows, fists, knees, and feet rained chops down on his head and neck, and the creature in his arms disappeared, jerked away by one of the others. Leery snarled and lashed out, batting one of the child-sized things through the air, and the other one turned and ran. The one he'd captured and lost ran away, hand in hand with his rescuer. Leery sprang to his feet, but even as he did so, his attackers disappeared with the sound of bursting balloons. He whirled in a circle, eyes seeking any movement, pulling air in through his nose.

He walked toward Dru, staring at the doors to the hall, though his nose told him there was no one out there. He regained his human form as he reached Dru's side. "They're all gone," he said. "No more cinnamon smell out there or in here."

Dru nodded, then looked him up and down. With a small smile, she let the glowing blue rune set fade and surveyed the mess made of the room. Corpses in various states littered the ground in front of the coolers.

Leery followed her gaze. "Looks like they only wanted the vampires," he said. He jerked his chin at the overturned exam table. "And the stake from LaSalle. What were those things?"

"I'm guessing here, but I'd say they were some species of Drow."

"But the Drow are nothing more than stories used to scare kids into behaving. Right?"

"Maybe now," said Dru with a shrug. "Not always."

II

Van Helsing frowned as they recounted the tale of their fight in the ME's workroom. She narrowed her eyes at Leery's description of the one he'd momentarily captured, then shook her head. "Drow," she spat. "I thought we'd seen the last of them in the mid-1700s."

"No such luck," said Leery.

"And how many of them were there?"

"I don't know. More than four," said Dru. "Some got caught in my spell, but at least three made it through, and they freed the one Leery had subdued."

"They never leave any of their kind behind," said the lieu. "Even the injured ones disappear when you look away."

"Why would they care about dead vampires?"

Epatha shook her head slowly. "There's no telling with those funkers. But if the Drow are invading the locus, we're up the flue, I promise you that."

"What do you want us to do, Lieu?" asked Leery.

"Keep on the murders. None of that is Drow style, so whatever the Drow did in the morgue, you can bet they did it for someone else."

"Who?"

"Don't you think if I knew that we'd be headed out to nab the dab cove?" She rolled her eyes and whirled around to face the search area again. "Follow the bodies. Liz says all of the vampires were Dead Set."

"Right, Lieu," said Leery. "We've got the CBI looking for Marlow."

"But what about the elves?" asked Dru. "They aren't in the Set."

Van Helsing sighed. "Yeah. Follow the stakes. Follow the magic that bound LaSalle's body together. Find out why the killer needs the bodies in the first place." She glanced at Dru. "Hendrix is working on all the identifications."

12

The sun had started its slow slide toward the western horizon by the time Bryant Wheelbarrowx and Regina Deal had a location for Marlow. And by the time Leery and Dru drove all the way out to Greenwich, the horizon had turned fifty shades of orange. Leery pulled in behind Bryant's pink monstrosity and put the cruiser in park. Coffee in hand, he and Dru climbed in the back seat of the Cube. "This is too nice a place for Marlow," said Leery.

Bryant pointed at the pale-yellow farmhouse with the hedge-wrapped yard sitting astride the mild bend in Elm Street. "And yet that's his house."

"Huh," said Leery. "I'd have pegged him for one of the more ostentatious jobs over by the bay."

"Nope," said Regina.

"SERT is staging at the local police airfield," said Bryant. "They'll do the takedown, then take Marlow back to Manhattan."

"Uh...then why did we schlep all the way out here?" asked Leery.

"Two reasons. First, after they cart him away, we can search the place. And second, there's a coffee shop down the road that I think you'll like."

"Coffee shop? Why didn't you say so? We could've met there and skipped all the cloak and dagger."

"This way we're close if something pops off," said Regina, fingering the edge on one of her knives. "And who said we want to skip the dagger part?"

13

A rhythmic thunder filled the night. Brilliant spotlights split the sky, bathing Marlow's house in white light, and ropes fell from the helicopters. Eight figures slid down the lines wearing all-black uniforms devoid of markings except the SERT and CBI patches decorating opposite shoulders. Each team member snaking down the lines carried wands, charms, and fetishes—everything they needed to make war on a vampire.

The SERT agents dropped from their lines a few feet above Marlow's yard, then sprinted for the house, flattening themselves against the pale-yellow clapboards. The one in the lead gave a nod, and a burly orc stepped out of the shadow of the house and the helos banked away. The orc leveled a geegaw at the door. With an atomic-green flash, the front door of the house exploded inward with an ear-splitting crash.

The shamans made entry in single file, the burly orc shaman in the lead. As they disappeared inside, a spout of black smoke leaked from one of the second-floor windows. It transformed into the shape of a swarm of locusts, and Regina pointed at it with the mirror-bright tip of her knife. "Right there," she said.

Bryant nodded and lifted his portable radio to his lips. "Wheelbarrowx to Blackfire. You owe me ten bucks."

"Roger."

The basso thump of the lead helicopter pounded down on them as it swept in and hovered over the smoke, dispersing it groundward. Regina and Bryant sprang from the car—followed a moment later by Leery and Dru—and sprinted into the downdraft of the helo as it decreased altitude, washing them all with its downdraft and sun-bright spotlight, and pressing the black smoke into a thin layer against the pavers of Marlow's drive.

"Give it up, Marlow," cried Regina, a silvered dagger in each hand. They surrounded the puff of smoke, each taking one of the cardinal points and standing ready.

Bryant held four fingers up to the helicopter and it banked away. "C'mon, drongo. You're caught."

The smoke gathered, mounding up like a pile of iron filings, and a mouth formed near the top. "Fuck off, noddy." The voice was thick with an Australian twang.

"Right, right," said Bryant. "But you *are* caught.

"Ah, Your Royal Majesty," said the smoke, the voice taking on cultured English tones.

Dru dipped her head. "Marlow." She chopped her hand through the air. "This display cheapens you, sir."

"Well, we can't have that." The smoke swirled and grew taller, and the moment when the smoke became thick black velvet swathing fish-belly white flesh passed without Leery's notice. Marlow swirled into a bow, his cape wafting out behind him, his hand extended to take Dru's. With a shrug, she placed her hand in his, and he kissed her knuckles. "Your Grace," Marlow murmured. He straightened, his gaze flicking toward Bryant with a momentary sneer before coming to rest on Regina and her knives. He sniffed. "Put them away, dear. Silver is so distasteful." His nostrils twitched, and he whirled to stare daggers at Leery. "And *you*. I should have known."

"Yeah, you really should have," said Leery.

With a disdainful shake of his head, Marlow turned his back on Leery and gave Dru his full attention. "Your Grace, I'd much rather have renewed our acquaintance in a more jovial setting. A party, filled with others of our kind, with libations and other comforts close to hand."

"I've got some coffee in the car," said Leery.

"I'm sure," said Dru. "But my attendance at Daisy Deen's party was no more than an undercover operation. The Dead Set is not an organization I wish to be associated with."

"Ah. Hercule's influence, no doubt." He placed a long, thin finger across his lips, his fingertip resting against the side of his nose as he gazed at her. "There are more things in heaven and Earth than are dreamt of in your father's philosophy."

"I'm afraid you don't understand that quote," said Leery after clearing his throat. "When Shakespeare wrote the word 'your,' he didn't mean in Horatio's philosophy. Instead, he meant a more generalized sense of your. Think of it as 'the,' instead. It was Hamlet rejecting the limits of science, a reassertion of the sovereignty of Christianity, a call for a return—"

"Yes, yes," said Marlow in a tone that made his disinterest clear. "Say what you will of misunderstood grammar, but I was present when Hamlet debuted, wolf. Can you say the same?"

Bryant stepped forward, holding a pair of silvered cuffs. "We will have plenty of time to argue about the Bard back in Manhattan."

"Oh, must we?" asked Marlow. "I've grown to detest the City."

"Oh, we must," said Leery, stepping forward and grabbing Marlow's forearms. The vampire tried to jerk his arms away but stopped struggling when Leery growled deep in his chest. He brought the vampire's wrists together. "Slap on the cuffs, Wheelbarrowx."

"Good job," said a woman behind him.

After the cuffs snicked shut, Leery glanced over his shoulder. "Oh, hello, Fanny!"

"Oriscoe," she said with a nod. "Nice work, but I'll take control of the prisoner from here."

"Sure." Leery stepped away from Marlow and gave the leader of the SERT team space.

Fanny stepped up close to Marlow's back and took hold of the chain linking his wrists together. "Come on, then, Marlow. Let's get you back to New York City."

"Must we?"

"I'm afraid we must." She turned him away from the four of them and led him back toward the helicopter sitting on his back lawn.

"Now," said Leery, clapping his hands together and rubbing them briskly, "about that coffee shop."

14

Leery filed into the precinct house behind Dru, Bryant, and Regina, looking down at the small cup of coffee he carried with a peculiar expression. "Are you sure *this* is their largest cup? I can't see how a place calling itself a coffee shop can get away with such a farce."

"It's sixteen ounces, Oriscoe," said Bryant with an air of longsuffering. "That *is* a large coffee."

"If you're a girl, maybe. And I don't mean a woman. I mean a twelve-year-old girl."

Bryant sighed and shook his head. "But the taste, Oriscoe? Isn't the taste of the coffee grand?"

"I really can't say, Wheelbarrowx. Anything served in such diminutive quantities can taste good. You really need a lot of something to see if it's good."

Bryant shook his head again. "Try to do something nice..."

"Oh, I appreciate it, Wheelbarrowx. It's hard to find good coffee shops close by."

"Connecticut is close by?" asked Regina with a quirky smile, and Leery shrugged.

They trooped into the elevator and rode up to their floor. Leery stepped out and shook his empty cup. "Coffee, anyone? I'll make it fresh."

Bryant pinched the bridge of his nose and Regina chuckled. "You need to see someone, Oriscoe," she said.

"For what?" Leery shook his head and glanced at Dru. "Ruined?"

Dru nodded, trying not to let her smile grow too wide.

"There you are!" said Van Helsing from thin air.

Regina jumped, one hand flicking one side of her coat open, her other hand racing toward the hilt of a throwing knife underneath. "Oh! Lieutenant..." She shook her head.

"Sorry, I didn't mean to startle anyone," said Epatha, coalescing in front of them. "Fanny Blackfire delivered your suspect an hour ago."

Dru nodded. "Bryant wanted to show Leery a new coffee shop in Greenwich."

Epatha quirked her eyebrow at Wheelbarrowx. "Well, ain't you a *gulpin?*"

"I have no idea what that means," said Bryant.

"And it's probably better that way," called Leery from the coffeemaker.

"Will I ever remember his ears?" muttered Van Helsing.

"Don't see why, Lieu. Dru doesn't remember them, either."

Van Helsing closed her eyes a moment, then shook her head. "Someone get in there."

Dru nodded and turned toward the interview room. "Observation is through there," she said to Regina and Bryant. She walked into the interview room, pausing at the door to take in the scene Marlow had so carefully constructed.

The vampire sat with his chair facing away from the door on a forty-five-degree angle, one leg crossed over the opposing knee, his velvet cape draped just so, the moonlight filtering through the grate over the window and illuminating his face. "Your Grace," he said, bowing his head for a moment. He picked at an imaginary piece of lint and sniffed. "I've been kept waiting."

"Sorry about that. Traffic," said Dru. She walked around the table and sat in one of the chairs there, scooching up to the edge of the seat and folding her hands on the table, forcing Marlow to either crane his neck or turn to see her.

The old vampire closed his eyes in a slow blink and sighed. When he opened his eyes, he stood and dragged the chair around, letting the brass feet of the chair screech against the old wooden floor of the station. He sank gracefully to the chair and cocked his head at Dru. "Tell me, Your Grace, will your...*partner*...be joining us?"

"Leery? Yes, of course. Any moment now."

They both glanced at the door for a moment, but it remained firmly closed. "Ah, well," said Marlow. "Dramatic entrances are much more easily managed in fiction." He spread his hands. "Tell me, Princess, to what do I owe this grand honor of being wrenched from my bed and dragged across state lines—by the CBI no less—and dropped into this hovel?"

Dru nodded once. "Antoine LaSalle is dead."

"Well, of *course*—"

"*True-death*," said Dru. "In fact, his immortal coil is no more."

"Gone back to the dust, eh?" Marlow lifted an eyebrow. "The old bastard finally grew bored enough with the goings-on to give up the ghost?"

"I'm afraid not," said Dru. "He was staked, then buried head down in Central Park."

The single tremor in Marlow's left eyebrow gave away his shock.

Leery banged through the door to the observation room, slamming the door into the wall with his elbow. "And, no, don't bring that Drow in until I tell you!" he yelled over his shoulder. He hooked the door with his heel and kicked it shut with a bang. "So hard to find competent cops these days," he muttered. He glanced at Dru and tipped a wink, disproving Marlow's assertion about dramatic entrances. "The old bloodsucker talking yet?" he demanded.

"Drow?" murmured Marlow.

"Eh?" said Leery, sliding into his chair and passing a cup of coffee to Dru. "Drow? When was the last time anyone saw one of them?"

Marlow lifted his shoulders. "The last time I saw one was in 1747. I take it you've seen one since?"

"When was the last time you *hired* a Drow?" asked Leery.

Again, Marlow shrugged his thin shoulders. "1747. It didn't go as planned."

"You sure about that, Marlow?"

"One remembers dealing with the Drow," said Marlow with a smirk.

"Who gains from LaSalle's death?" asked Dru in a quiet voice.

"Gains, Your Grace? No one gains when great leaders fall," said Marlow.

"Come on, Marlow. You no more think LaSalle was a great leader than I think you're Cinderella."

"It's true that I don't have the toes for crystal slippers," said Marlow. "And, if you must know the truth, I did think LaSalle was an idiot, but as one of the leaders of the Dead Set—"

"*One* of the leaders?" asked Dru.

Marlow glanced at her but only shrugged. "The Movement is beyond the scope of any one mind, Your Grace."

"Then LaSalle had to pay the price for his transgressions, right?" asked Leery.

Marlow shook his head. "No."

"No?"

"No. LaSalle beat you, beat your prosecutor. That alone is reason enough to ignore whatever transgressions you imagine he made."

Leery looked at Dru and shrugged.

"Who were LaSalle's enemies?" she asked.

"Antoine made many enemies," mused Marlow. "Though none worth mentioning. None with the power and the guts to go up against him."

A knock sounded on the mirrored glass, and both detectives looked at it and grimaced.

"That, I imagine, is Jeffery," said Marlow with a smile. "It was nice seeing you again, Princess. Perhaps next time, you should call instead of all this theater." He stood, glanced at the mirror, and straightened his black velvet brocade vest.

The door to the squad room banged open, and Jeffery DeRothenberg stood in the doorway. His caustic gaze flicked past Leery and Dru, then came to rest on Marlow. "Come, Marlow," he said, holding out his hand. "They have less than nothing."

Marlow shrugged and smiled at Dru. "There's nothing to have. I had nothing to do with poor Antoine's death."

"Help us, Marlow," she said. "Help us figure out who killed Antoine LaSalle."

DeRothenberg's lip curled. "No, Detective. You do your job without involving my client."

Marlow smiled and cocked his head to the side. "If you'd come to me and asked for my help, I might have, but after raiding my home, capturing me on the lawn like some common criminal..." He spread his hands. "I think I will leave." He turned and led DeRothenberg out of the squad room.

"Well, at least we didn't infringe on his rights," said Leery.

"Progress," said Dru with a wan smile.

Van Helsing drifted through the wall of the observation room. "Hendrix just called. She's identified the elf victims."

"On our way," said Leery.

15

Leery and Dru rode the elevator in the building sixteen blocks from Liz's usual workspace and got off into a brightly lit hallway. They walked around for a few minutes, following room numbers until they found her temporary lab. Leery held the door for Dru, then followed her inside.

"Thanks for wrecking my lab!" snapped Hendrix.

"That wasn't us. It was the Drow," said Leery.

"Drow? They're a myth!"

"Hey, that's what I thought about werewolves," said Leery. "Evidently the Drow disappeared in the mid-eighteenth century. And now they're back."

"You learn something new every day," grumped Liz.

"Come on, Hendrix. You know we wouldn't stage a battle in your lab by our choice."

"You, Oriscoe, might do *anything* that makes my life more complicated. For proof, I refer you to these bodies that keep arriving—*despite* an attack by the mysterious Drow!"

"Yeah, about that," said Leery. "You see, I told them to send you the bodies when they'd only found a few..."

"And I suppose you'd have sent them elsewhere if you'd known?"

"Well..." Leery glanced at Dru for help but found none. "No."

"No." Hendrix sighed. "Well, I've got a couple of things to show you, even though I hate you."

"The job comes first."

"Shut up. First, I identified four of these elves, and there's a pattern that LaSalle fits right into."

"Oh yeah?"

"Yes, or I wouldn't have wasted my breath saying all that. They're all criminals."

Leery arched one eyebrow.

"LaSalle, you know his record." Liz turned and walked over to several gurneys pressed against the wall. She lifted the sheet from one. On the gurney lay a pale-skinned elf with white-blond hair. "Alfred Guthfiddur."

Leery whistled. "Leader of the Arcane Brotherhood?"

"The very same," said Liz. She moved to the next gurney and flipped the sheet back to reveal a swarthy-skinned Svartalfar with midnight hair bordering on blue and scars that crisscrossed his body. "Byurn Leefsmathur of the Dautha Glott." She pointed at the next gurney. "Leader of the Shadow guild." She moved her finger to the next. "Leader of the Svartalfar branch of the Black Hand."

Leery whistled again. "All powerful elves."

"And no doubt protected as well as LaSalle," murmured Dru. "Except for Alfred, there, all are assassins in their own right."

"And Alfred's a mercenary...a warrior mage."

"And they were all taken unawares," said Liz. "No defensive wounds."

"How's that possible?" asked Dru.

"And then there's this." Liz moved to Alfred's corpse and pried his jaws open. She picked up a small LED flashlight and shined it into his throat.

Leery stepped closer and peered into the elf's mouth. "What is that? A medallion?"

"Amulet," said Liz, letting go of the elf and stepping toward the countertop running along the opposite wall. "I used an arthroscope to take pictures. I can't extract the amulets."

"No, if they're like the stakes, they're enchanted in place," said Dru. They crossed the room and stood looking down at the runes inscribed on the amulet's face. "I'm not a hundred percent certain, but I think those are very similar to what we saw on the stakes."

Liz nodded and uncovered another photograph—this one of the stake lodged in LaSalle's chest. "There are new runes on the amulets, but there are enough exact matches to be certain they are from the same alphabet."

"Proto-Earmite," said Leery.

"Uh…"

"He means Elamite. Proto-Elamite and Enochian."

"Yeah, that's what Vinny Gonofrio said." Leery straightened and looked across the room at the corpses. "I'm not sure those fine gentlemen are safe here."

"It's a secure building," said Liz with a shrug. "Guards in the halls, alarms on all the doors."

"Still," he said. "Do you know the cause of death?"

"That's the really strange part."

Leery cocked an eyebrow.

"By all appearances, someone stole their breath."

"Uh…" Leery glanced at Dru.

Dru dimpled and chuckled. "Not like that, Leery," she said.

Liz grinned with one side of her face. "No. Not at all like the colloquial meaning of the phrase. I mean this literally, Oriscoe. Every time they drew breath, someone stole it before their lungs could process it. Then, as these elves expired, I expect those amulets were inserted to bind them in the same manner as the vampires."

"So, you're telling us someone in New York City is stealing the souls of criminal leaders?"

"Yes, and it's not Dru's uncle."

16

By the time they rode the elevator back downstairs and got in the car, it was going on nine-thirty. Dru called Van Helsing on speakerphone as they sat letting the car warm up. "Yes, Lieu, that is what I said. They are all leaders of criminal organizations, and the killer enchanted amulets to bind the lifeforce from them in the same way LaSalle's was bound."

"That…doesn't make sense to me. Were the elves undead?"

"No, Lieu," said Leery. "But they *were* elves. Magical beings."

"Ah," said Van Helsing. "And are their organizations linked in any way?"

"The Black Hand, Guild of Shadows, Dautha Glott, and the Arcane Brotherhood."

"Then, no," said Epatha. "Most peculiar."

"And the Dead Set wouldn't employ any of those organizations," said Dru.

"Then the only overlap is their unrelated criminal acts."

"Looks that way, Lieu," said Leery. "And what's worse is that by all appearances, the perp is going about this systematically. Killing all vampires, then switching to elves."

"Or vice versa. But how could any one person know the deeds of all these different people?"

"My Uncle Luci knows. There must be other magical creatures with the same power."

"True. The Angels of Judgment come to mind."

"Right," said Leery. "And how many other religions have a similar role? Anubis, for instance."

"Does it strike you as odd that a being with such power would stoop to murder and vigilantism?"

"Not really," said Dru. "Uncle Luci is cast as a punisher, after all."

"True, but he has the good grace to await death, not cause it."

"Still, Lieu, the principle stands. Many cultures, many religions empower a being with the power to peer into our hearts and see our deeds, then make that being punish everyone for their sins."

"So, tomorrow, we look into who's visiting Manhattan, who's scheduled to be here soon, and who has just left us. Look for overlap with enchanting, Proto-Elamite, and this Yoltomta character."

"We're on it, Lieu," said Leery.

"Then get home and get some rest. I want you both in here early tomorrow morning, bright-eyed and bushy-tailed."

They signed off and sat staring out over the hood of the Crown Vic, looking at the pretty lights decorating the street. "Well, I guess I'll drop you at home," said Dru.

Leery sighed. "Yeah, first night back in my own digs and all that."

Dru put the car in gear and pulled away from the curb. "Yeah," she said after a moment. "First night of freedom."

"That's true."

"And you've laid in supplies?"

"What I need, yeah."

"Don't forget to feed your wolf."

"No, I won't. I've got the butcher down the street setting me up with a box."

"Good," said Dru.

They rode in silence as Dru piloted the car across the city. She pulled up in front of his building, and Leery glanced out the window, peering up at the dark mound of brick. "Smaller than I remember," he murmured. He relaxed and looked her way, then put his hand on the door handle. "Well, I guess I'll—"

"You could call if—" said Dru at the same moment, then they both laughed.

"Yeah, you, too," said Leery. "Can call, I mean."

Dru nodded, and their gazes drifted together. They sat that way for a minute or more, then Leery lifted his hand and reached toward her. He seemed to run out of gas before he touched her cheek, and he let his hand fall on her shoulder in an awkward pat. "Get some rest," he muttered as though she were the one getting out. Then he opened the door and got out and went upstairs.

Inside his apartment, Leery took off his coat, laid it across a chair, and grinned. He went to the refrigerator for a cold beer, then came back and stood in the middle of his living room, smiling, and thinking about Lucifer's place.

He shook his head and grabbed his remote, flicking on the television and then standing stock-still staring at it without making sense of the images. He dropped the remote on the couch, took another swig of beer, and walked into his bedroom, noticing for the first time how tiny it was, how tiny his double bed looked.

Turning his back on the bedroom, he noticed for the first time how claustrophobic his living room was. Low ceilinged, long and narrow, overstuffed with furniture—too much furniture for a single man. He grimaced at it, then picked up the remote and flipped through the channels without seeing them. He sat on the couch, beer in one hand, remote hanging loosely from the other, and leaned his head back on the couch. "Freedom," he muttered.

He snapped off the television, put both the beer and the remote on the coffee table, then stood and donned his coat. He looked around, his gaze drifting without purpose, then turned and left his crackerbox apartment on the Upper West Side.

17

Dru pulled the car up onto the sidewalk and grinned sideways at Leery. He pointed at the C3 parked at the end of the block. Outside, darkness still reigned in the early morning sky, but it wasn't too early for Epatha Van Helsing. She appeared as soon as they got out of the car.

"It's about time," she said. Her glance flicked back and forth between them for half a minute. "Why didn't you answer your phone, Oriscoe?"

"Uh, sorry, Lieu. Battery was dead and I forgot to plug it in."

"Figures."

"I took the car home last night. I ran by and picked him up."

"It was faster this way," said Leery.

Epatha arched an eyebrow. "I didn't ask. And don't sell me a dog, Oriscoe. Dru had to cross town, pick you up, then come halfway back here, didn't she? How's that faster than you coming on your own?"

"Uh. No cabs this early," said Leery, ducking his head.

"Uh-huh," said Van Helsing. "Well, never mind all that for now—we'll get back to it later. At the precinct. But can you guess what happened to those elf stiffs?"

"The Drow stole them?" asked Leery.

"Right and fly, Oriscoe. But, this time, Hendrix was smart. She attached a tracker to each one. They are in a warehouse two blocks down the street." She pointed at a building in the other direction from the command, control, and communication trailer.

"Are we part of the raid?" asked Leery, his hand resting on his belt buckle.

"Well, I didn't call you down here in the middle of the night so you could giggle and flirt like a pair of schoolyard lovers."

"Lieu—"

"Save it, Oriscoe. Time to go to work." She pointed at the command center. "SWAT will breach in ten minutes. You two are in the second wave. Be ready. Queue up by the C3."

"Right."

Van Helsing winked out, leaving Dru and Leery standing in the cold. Leery sighed, opened the passenger door, and sat half-in, half-out of the car. He slipped out of his shoes, loosening his belt as he did so.

"Don't you think you should wait?"

"Nah," said Leery. "My fur is warmer than this coat, and this way I can have dry, warm clothes when it's all over." He dropped his shoes and belt onto the backseat, then loosened his tie.

"So, no flirting," said Dru with a grin.

"With Epatha skulking around, maybe that's for the better."

Dru's grin faded a little as Leery pulled off the rest of his clothes and stepped naked into the light snow. He flash-transformed to his wolf, Lucifer's enchanted amulet produced the black woolen hat to cover his fur-knitted *yarmulke*, his *payot* long and glossy. He glanced down at Dru and grunted a soft bark from deep in his chest. She reached up and patted his furry arm, then turned and walked toward the C3 trailer.

18

Ten minutes later, they followed a whisper-quiet line of therianthropes as the SWAT units approached the warehouse. The words "Kerstman Industries" blazed from the warehouse walls in three-foot-tall fancy-script letters.

The warehouse was dark, and inside, nothing moved. Dru and Leery stopped with the rest of the second wave half-a-block out from the warehouse's office door. The therianthropes moved forward, joined by the servitor warriors who merely appeared out of thin air.

The column of SWAT officers split into entry teams, each stacking up on their assigned doors, then as brilliant white light speared down from above to illuminate the entire exterior of the building, they slammed doors aside and rushed into the darkness.

A soft whine escaped Leery's lips as he shuffled his feet, wanting to go, go, GO. Dru patted his arm, and that made it a little better. "Almost time," she whispered.

Flashes of light exploded from the interior of Kerstman Industries, followed by the clattering cacophony of multiple small battles, and Leery could stand it no longer. With a howl, he charged at the main entrance, followed by the other Claws from the second wave, and then, farther back, by their Warders. His focus narrowed to a single-minded desire to get inside and find an enemy.

He sprinted toward the breached door in a crouch, then dropped to all fours as he swept inside, hackles up, senses on full alert. The scent-trace of the main door's entry team went straight down a long double-width hallway, but the odor of cinnamon and cloves came from the right—from a smaller hallway with office doors peppering its length.

With a howl he hoped Dru could hear, he leaned to the right, claws digging into the rough industrial carpet under his paws, and peeled off the main column of second-wave Claws. He slowed from an all-out sprint, then slowed again, ears perked forward. He stopped in the mouth of the hall, yellow-eyed glower stabbing down its length.

The office doors were all closed, and no sound issued from that side of the building at all, yet the strong scent of cinnamon blasted through his nostrils like the blue flame of an oxy-acetylene torch. His gaze flicked to the nameplates on the doors: Nicholas Sinter, Martin Kristkind, Othidn Vetramathur, Dun Che Lao Ren, Hoteiosho Kurosho, Ded Moroz, and Einar Julenissen. The names meant nothing to Leery, and his wolf-half urged him on, as the cinnamon scent wormed its way into his brain, demanding action, calling for combat. A low rumble sounded from his chest as he took a careful step into the hallway's umbra.

19

Dru followed Leery's mad charge toward the building, wishing, not for the first time, that she could match his speed. Despite the gifts of her birth, she didn't have his length of leg, and she couldn't match his long, loping strides.

It had nothing to do with the three-inch heels on her boots.

As she ran, she crafted a rune set in dark navy blue with shimmering mercury lines, activated it, and lay it on the crown of her head. It settled around her like a translucent blue shroud, then faded from view. She began another set, this time choosing maroon and acid-yellow lines. It was a complicated pattern, but one she hoped would subdue a Drow.

She crossed the threshold into the warehouse lobby just in time to see Leery's tail disappear into the murk on her right. She skidded to a stop after clearing the path for the Warders following their Claws straight into the warehouse. She muttered in the *Lingua Tenebris Lacuna* and empowered her rune set, holding it gingerly in the palm of her right hand. With her left, she began a rune set that would augment her night vision, her gaze bouncing between it and the dark hallway.

20

Leery crept down the hall, the pads of his paws barely registering sound on the industrial carpet beneath him. The doors remained closed and still, even as he passed the first of them, but the mélange of cinnamon, clove, and herd animal grew stronger—as though Drow rushed to stand behind the doors, stacking up as the SWAT members had outside. With a force of will, he stilled the low growl in his chest and continued past the next door, unconsciously straying to the far edge of the hall and keeping his gaze glued to the door as he passed.

The silence through which he padded unnerved him. He *knew* Drow hid behind the closed doors. He knew it as surely as he knew Dru would soon come behind him, her spells at the ready to aid, protect, and heal him. But the absolute silence belied that instinctual knowledge and called the overpowering amalgamation of spicey and earthy scents a lie.

He realized he was growling again and forced himself to stop. *Answer stealth with stealth,* he told his wolf. He peered into the gloom, seeing a last door, one he couldn't see from the lobby, nestled as it was in a narrow alcove to his left. The nameplate on the door read D. Kerstman, Proprietor.

He sank low to the ground, his belly fur almost brushing the floor, the tips of his claws penetrating the thick carpet with each slow step, his tail rigid behind him, his ears folded back flat on his head.

As he approached the last door, he narrowed his eyelids and opened his jaws wide.

21

As the night vision spell took hold, Dru crept forward, barely able to look at the shimmering red runes throbbing in her right palm. The cloying stink of cinnamon, cloves, and animal den clogged her nostrils and brought bile to the back of her throat by its olfactory power alone. She paused to read the names from the doors, finding them strange.

Ahead, she saw Leery creeping forward, close to the left wall, crouched low—so low he seemed almost to crawl on his belly—and she knew his posture from their year together: hunting wolf. She took his example and drifted to the left of the hallway until her left shoulder brushed the wall. She paused to bring another spell to the ready, this one consisting of nineteen blue runes connected with golden lines. She muttered the activation phrase in the *Verba Patiendi* but didn't send it on its way, not wanting to distract Leery at a crucial moment.

As she passed the second door in the line, she heard a faint rustle, like rough cloth shifting on silk, and tensed, her gaze locking on the door opposite her. She stared at it with her augmented vision, watching the knob slowly turn.

22

His growl was back, rumbling away in his throat and chest like an unstoppable infernal engine. He padded closer to Kerstman's door, lips curling back to turn his growl into a snarl, the cinnamon, clove, and animal-pen stink burning in his nostrils, almost strong enough to send him scuttling backward on their own merit.

But his eyes detected a glint of stray light on the doorknob, and it was turning counterclockwise at a plodding pace. His legs bunched beneath him, and he rocked side to side in short, apprehensive arcs, settling his weight on his paws, preparing to spring. Saliva dripped from his open maw, and his eyelids narrowed to mere slits.

Behind him, he heard Dru gasp, and at the same moment, the latch on Kerstman's door clicked, and Leery sprang, aiming for chest height on a normal man, neck stiffening for the impact with the door, head drifting toward the widening crack between the door and the jamb.

23

Dru gasped as the door across from her cracked open. From the end of the hall, she heard Leery launching himself through the air with a savage snarl, but her gaze was locked on the widening strip of darkness between her door and the doorjamb. She flung the blue rune set toward Leery, and, at the same time, she whipped her right palm forward, as though presenting the rune set in there, acid-yellow blaze fighting maroon fire for dominance.

The door slammed open, and a flurry of darkly clad, child-sized bodies poured out. At the same time, the maroon and yellow rune set on her palm bounced once, then darted forward as if by its own accord, and the Drow leaped back, hands flung up to ward off the runes' brilliance.

A symphony of snarling and growling erupted down the hall, but Dru kept her sight centered on her attackers, calculating their distance from the runes. At the last moment, she squeezed her eyes shut and turned her face away.

24

Leery slammed into the door, driving it open with explosive force. He rode it inward a moment, then lunged away from it, angling through the widening gap, jaws open, ready to bite, ready to slash and tear. He sensed—rather than saw—the horde of Drow huddled on the inside of the door, some sprawled on their backs from the force of his attack, others springing away. He landed gracefully among them, claws slashing, fangs tearing, using his weight to knock more of the short creatures down, away, back.

Then—too late—he saw the flash of silver.

25

Kaleidoscopic colors exploded on the other side of Dru's eyelids, and despite their protection, she cringed away, moving down the hall toward Leery by the feel of her shoulder on the wall. Behind her, thin wavering screams sounded as her spell pulsed detonations into the small office beyond the door.

The Drow lying in wait in that office had no chance as the maroon tentacles of eldritch power swept through the room like water shot from a rotating sprinkler, hurling tiny bodies against the wall, then smaller acid-yellow tentacles snapped out and bound their wrists and ankles.

The barnyard and spice odor redoubled as the next door in line sprang open, and Drow poured out of it, reaching, grasping, snarling.

26

Leery pulled back against the wall, backing away from the child-sized silver weapons clutched in tiny pale-skinned fists, snarling and snapping at the ones who dared get too close. A flicker of silvery-blue shone momentarily in the corner of his eye, and then Dru's rune set settled around him like a mantle. The Drow scattered back, warding their eyes with open hands. The power of the runes seeped into Leery, energizing his neural pathways, filling his muscles with potential, swelling them, bulking him up—much as had occurred in his brief fight with Lucifer so many months ago, but this time, he didn't grow taller, only bulkier.

He howled to let Dru know the spell had found him, then snarled with menace at the gaggle of Drow before him. Some—the brave among them—brandished their silver axes, their silver short swords, their silver daggers, and stood their ground. But most of them fell back before him, hiding behind the desk, the credenza, the massive upholstered executive chair. His snarl deepened, roughened, became a thing of anger and vengeance rather than a warning, and he stepped toward the Drow defying him, stiff-legged and ready to fight.

27

Dru stumbled back, fleeing the onslaught of ferocious child-like faces, the fists, the silver weapons, fiercely hacking runes out of the air with both hands, her desperate gaze shifting toward the end of the hall, hoping to see Leery loping toward her, but there was only darkness. "Leery!" she cried as the Drow advanced and encircled her.

As their malevolent circle began to constrict, she finished a rune set of arterial red connected with lines as black as death. She empowered the spell with a bark of spidery *Lingua Tenebris Lacuna*, even as her expensive boots lifted off the carpet, and her eyes flared red to match the runes. She flung the rune set against the press of black-clothed Drow and cried Leery's name, her voice like thunder.

28

Leery crouched to spring, ignoring the flashing silver blades, his gaze boring into the little almond-shaped eyes of the Drow opposing him, his snarl sounding like a furious pack rather than a single wolf. But then he heard Dru call his name, and he paused, head cocked.

As though he'd been waiting for a signal, the Drow standing defiantly close raised his ax and sprang.

The flash of the blade drew Leery's attention—and his wrath. His head darted forward, and one vicious snap left the Drow screaming and short one hand.

Thunder filled the hall outside—his name once more cried by Dru in the throaty vestiges of her power. With a savage bark, Leery whirled and hurled himself back into the hall, a howl reverberating through the enclosed space.

Wolves throughout the building answered his cry, followed by the cries of Warders wanting to know where help was needed. Leery charged down the hall, snarling and howling, each in turn, ignoring the Drow behind him, ignoring the Drow pouring from the other offices—unless they threatened to slow him. Those Drow he grabbed in his jaws and shook as he ran, flinging away their rag-doll bodies at the next group in his way.

Ahead, brilliant red and magenta explosions of eldritch magic went off, cratering the walls and flinging tiny black-clad bodies hither and yon. He squinted against the variegated onslaught but didn't turn his face away, didn't lift his gaze from Dru's hovering body. Her eyes stabbed the darkness, twin daggers of vermillion destruction, and her voice thundered in the *Lingua Tenebris Lacuna*, calling down death on the Drow threatening her.

The sea of bodies between them seemed to be growing, thickening, despite Leery's best efforts. He snarled louder, howled more and more desperately, snapped and slashed at the little bodies, but still, they slowed him. He lunged into the air, springing over their heads, ignoring the burning streaks of pain along his flanks as he tore through them.

Dru's scarlet gaze washed over him, and orange lightning slashed into the crowd of

Drow accosting him. The air filled with spidery commands, words of destruction, words of power, words of command.

Leery snapped and bit, slashed with his claws, punched and kicked with his paws, roaring and howling, and slammed his weight from side to side, battering his way through the miasma of Drow-stink and of the Drow themselves.

A hot frenzy overtook him, and he gave in to it, allowing the whirling-dervish of claw and fang and killer instinct within him to take control. He twirled in place, sinking fangs here, slashing at a face there, shouldering small forms aside, tossing them away broken and bloodied. His snarls reached a fever-pitch crescendo, saw-blade ragged, branding-iron fervent, and above it all still, thundered Drusilla bat Agrat, Heir to the Throne of Gehenna, Thundering Angel of Righteous Wrath, Seductress, Desolator, Caller of Demons, Cold Caress of Darkest Night, Mistress of Runes, She of the Great and Terrible Name, and her terrible anger rained down on her enemies.

Other Claws, other Warders began to find them, fighting toward them from the lobby, and slowly, the Drow began to give up, disappearing with strings of rapid-fire pops.

As the press of Drow bodies dissipated, Dru turned her attention to Leery's wounds, dropping healing and invigorating spells on him. For his part, he still snarled at the Drow, even though the only ones left had no strength left with which to flee, to fight, or do more than lie in bloody heaps. Finally, as the last Drow was taken into custody, the whirling dervish inside him subsided, and he sank to his haunches at Dru's side, still panting but reveling in the strength of her spells. She rested a hand on his head. "Thank you for coming," she whispered.

If wolves could be said to shrug and smile, that's what Leery did.

29

Leery sighed and sank into his desk chair. He looked tired, but after the battle they'd fought, he had a right to be. The names on the doors in that hallway still bothered him, but not as much as the way the

Drow seemed to know they were coming. "I don't know, Lieu," he said. "If they knew the bodies were tagged, why stay with them?"

"And why take them to that particular warehouse? Chosen at random? With the trap they set in the offices?" Dru shook her head. "No, I don't buy that. Maybe it wasn't an ambush for Leery and me in particular, but it *was* an ambush."

"I'm not arguing that," said Van Helsing. "And I don't have a solution to this fifteen puzzle." She walked through the desks aligned between them. "Look, we have a few of the Drow. Let's interrogate them before they regain their energy and—" Leery's phone rang, and Epatha glared down at it.

"Oriscoe," he said as he picked it up. "Yeah, thanks loads, fellas." Then he sighed and hung up. He looked up at Epatha. "No one left to grill, Lieu. The last of the Drow just disappeared out of the transport van as it pulled up downstairs."

"Damn! I told those knuckleheads to hurry *and* to get them under antimagic wards." Van Helsing flickered like a strobe light. "You two could have left a few more intact!"

"We did, Lieu. They ported away the same as the ones we captured, just sooner."

Van Helsing grimaced and chopped a translucent hand through the air. "How are we supposed to solve this if the suspects can teleport away at will?"

"Those names... They must mean something," said Dru.

"Unless the warehouse was picked at random," said Leery.

Van Helsing glared down at him. "Well? What are you waiting for? Go find out!"

Leery sighed and grabbed the phone again. "On it, Lieu."

30

They pushed into the warmth of the Starbucks near 1PP, stomping the snow from their shoes and dusting it from their shoulders. Vinny lifted his gaze and looked around, then smiled when he saw Leery and Dru.

"Took you long enough," said Leery. "We had to come all the way down from the Two Seven."

"You complain a lot, you know that, Leery?" Vinny looked at Dru, showing her a small grin. "Besides, you shouldn't complain. Not today. I've found something."

"Yeah?" asked Leery after a slow draw on his *trenta*. "What's that, Vinny?"

"You're not going to believe it."

"Try me," said Leery with a grin of his own.

"Okay. You know I started with Yoltomta? I wanted to check old immigration records, genealogical stuff. And it worked. I found him, but he gave his name as Yol Tomta, two words, and he immigrated to this continent back in 1608." Vinny bounced his gaze back and forth between them for a moment, almost bouncing in his seat with excitement. Kathandra shook her head and smiled. "Guess what I found next."

"Look, Gonofrio—"

"Go on! Guess."

"You might as well," said Kathandra. "He's like a kid with this stuff."

"Fine. Next, you found out the year Yol Tomta died."

"That's right! But more important than that, I found out who inherited from Yol Tomta."

"Inherited?"

Vinny flapped a hand in the air. "Yeah. It wasn't the United States at that time, but the Covenancy was still represented here. Except there are no Covenancy records for Yol Tomta. At least not by that name. Like I said, there were Covenancy representatives in the Colonies, but without a governing body with immigration rules and all that..." Vinny shrugged. "Ask me who got his stuff. Go on, ask."

"Okay. Who'd he bequeath his slinky to?" asked Leery.

"Einar Julenissen. Another Norwegian name, though not Old Norse." He bounced his bright-eyed gaze between them again. "Guess who *he* left the slinky to."

"I have a feeling I'm not going to like the answer."

"Othidn Vetramathur." Vinny smiled and nodded as if anyone had said anything. "Know what that name means? It-it-it's Old Norse."

"No idea, Vinny. You're the one with all the languages."

"Yeah, I know. It means, 'Odin winter man.' I figure it might be a colloquialism for Odin, Father Winter."

Leery shook his head. "Look, Vinny, it's been—"

"Hear me out. Hear me out. This-this is *exciting*, Oriscoe!"

Leery sighed and took up his *trenta,* leaning back in his seat. "All ears, Vinny."

"Know who inherited from Father Winter?"

Leery shook his head and drank more coffee.

"You're not going to believe it."

"Not if I never *hear* it, Vinny."

"Right, right. Sorry. A man named Martin Kristkind."

"Wait," said Dru. "Are you sure?"

"Yeah. Why?"

Dru held up her hand and ticked the names off on her fingers. "Yol Tomta, Einar Julenissen, Othidn Vetramathur, Dun Che Lao Ren, Nicholas Sinter—"

"No, Dun Che Lao Ren comes later," said Vinny, but Kathandra shushed him, and he sat back, a glum frown forming on his lips.

"—Martin Kristkind, Hoteiosho Kurosho, Ded Moroz, and D. Kerstman. I bet all those names are on your list."

Vinny's frown grew. "Yeah, but you got the order wrong. After Martin Kristkind, Ded Moroz got the slinky. Then Nicholas Sinter, then, Hoteiosho Kurosho, one Dun Che Lao Ren, and finally, Dagmar Kerstman."

Leery looked at Dru and quirked his eyebrows. "*All* of them?"

Dru nodded.

"Wait. What are you two talking about? All of *whom?* What haven't you told me?" Vinny glanced at Kathandra, who rolled her eyes. "Us, I mean. It's not fair to withhold pertinent facts, guys."

"Relax, Vinny," said Leery. "We just learned them on this morning's raid."

"Right! I forgot. How'd that go?"

Leery waved it away. "All those names were found on offices in the warehouse of Kerstman Industries, D. Kerstman, Proprietor. Also found there, about six million Drow and a bunch of dead elves."

"Technically, the Drow *are* elves," said Vinny. "They come from the same home-realm and are thought to be parallel evolutionary branches."

"Thanks, Bill Nye," said Kathandra. "How does that help solve this case?"

Vinny glanced at her. "Well, maybe it doesn't, but it is interesting, right?" He looked at Leery. "Right?" He looked at Dru. "Right? Don't you find it interesting?"

"Well—" began Leery.

"But never mind that for now," said Vinny. "Want to know what's *really* interesting?"

"Well...sure," said Leery.

"Each one of those names...*all* of those names, they're other names for the being you call Santa Claus in this realm."

"I think you made a mistake there," said Leery. "I mean those Asian names are—"

"Dun Che Lao Ren, Chinese for 'Christmas Old Man.'" Vinny smiled at Leery. "Don't feel bad about that one, he's a relatively new thing over there."

"And the other one?"

"Japanese," said Vinny in a didactic tone. "A combination of a Buddhist monk Santa analog called Hoteiosho, and the name Santa Kurosho."

"What about Kerstman?"

"From the Dutch. De Kerstman, also known as Santa."

"Nicholas Sinter?"

Vinny's smile widened. "That's an interesting one—well, they're *all* interesting, but Nicholas Sinter is especially so. A combination of Sinterklass and Sint-Nicolaas, both from the Dutch tradition."

"Martin Kristkind?"

"Yeah, they got lazy there. Martin is a throw-away name. The real interest is Kristkind. 'Christ Child' auf Deutsch."

Kathandra waved her hand and sighed. "You might as well tell us about the last one."

"Ded Moroz? Originally a snow demon from Slavic mythology, but he evolved into Father Frost over time. Also known as the Russian Santa Claus."

"All this is"—Leery looked up, searching for the right thing to say—"interesting—"

"I know, right?" said Vinny, bouncing on his toes. "I love language."

"—but I'm not sure how it helps us."

"Don't you see?" asked Vinny, pointing at Leery with his outstretched hand, his leather-bound notebook tucked under his other arm. "They are *all* the same person, Leery."

"Right, I get that, Vinny. The question is, *which* person?"

"Oh. I thought it was obvious. Dagmar Kerstman is listed as the current proprietor of Kerstman Industries, right? He's your man."

31

Dru pulled the Crown Victoria up on the sidewalk outside a modern-looking high-rise on the corner of Madison Avenue and 80th Street, threading the car between the wall of the building and the young trees planted toward the edge of the narrow sidewalk. They got out and walked down 80th to the canopy protecting the building's entrance from the elements. The building's doorman gave them the once over, then lifted his hand like a traffic cop commanding them to stop.

"Relax, pal," said Leery as he pulled out his shield. "NYPD. Here on official business. Please tell me Dagmar Kerstman is at home."

The doorman shook his head. "I'm afraid you've missed him by a week."

"Traveling?"

"I was informed this morning that Mr. Kerstman passed away last week."

"Well, that's inconvenient?" muttered Leery.

"I should think so," said the doorman with a partially concealed frown. "Mr. Kerstman was a good man. He often went out of his way to make others happy. In fact, his entire business focused on this time of year. The Holidays, I mean. Did you know that he donated hundreds of thousands of dollars of toys to unfortunates? He also picked people randomly and paid off all their debts—*including* their mortgages." He shook his head. "Mr. Kerstman was a great man, Detective."

"No doubt," said Dru. "Did he have family?"

The doorman shrugged. "He had close friends." He glanced around, then leaned close. "*Elves*," he whispered.

"And Drow?" asked Leery.

"What are Drow?" asked the doorman.

"Never mind. Any idea who we can talk to about Mr. Kerstman's estate?"

The doorman shook his head. "No, sorry. You might try at his business. Kerstman Industries over on—"

"Thanks," said Leery, "but we were there last night. How about letting us into his apartment?"

"No, I'm sorry."

"Come on. What can it hurt?"

The doorman shook his head. "Sorry. To let you in without a proper warrant would mean my job. Building policies, you know."

"Sure. Thanks anyway."

Dru and Leery turned and walked back to the car. "Should we get the warrant?" she asked.

"Nah, the place is already swept clean. This is a planned event, this death. He's moving identities again. The only question is to who."

Dru thought for a moment. "We can check the other names."

Leery shook his head, a grim smile on his lips. "I don't think so. He knows we have them. He knows we're onto him. No, he'll burrow deep, lay low."

"Why don't we try other names for Santa Claus. Ones that didn't show up in Vinny's genealogy research."

"What are you, a detective or something?" Leery grinned at her. "Let's start with the obvious: good old Kris Kringle."

32

Leery sighed and pushed the laptop away from him. He grabbed his coffee mug, then grimaced down at the empty cup. "Who drank my coffee? I had a full cup here." He looked around the squad room suspiciously.

"You did," said Dru without looking up.

"Well, eliminate the obvious solutions to any problem, and what remains, no matter how unlikely, must be the answer," said Leery. "I probably drank the whole pot and will have to make a new one, right?"

"I have no doubt." She lifted her gaze from her laptop's screen and smiled. "Finding anything?"

"Besides my empty mug? Not really. Who knew they'd make a musical about the guy?"

"Uh—"

"And all the impersonators. They must make bank on Christmas parties."

"Uh. Bank?"

"Yeah. You know, moolah. Cash, Dru. I must have found at least two hundred of them in Gravel."

Dru rolled her eyes toward the ceiling and puffed out her cheeks. "That's not exactly what I meant by database searches, Leery."

Leery got up and walked toward the coffeemaker. "You're lucky we still have power. Or that Minnesota didn't break in half." He picked up the glass coffee pot and peered inside. "I knew it," he mumbled, then set his mug down next to the machine and walked toward the bathrooms. He only made it about halfway before his cell phone jangled "Never Gonna Give You Up." He juggled the still-hot coffee pot under his arm and pulled out his phone. "Oriscoe."

"Leery? Liz."

"Say hey, Hendrix. How's life in the new lab?"

"You mean the third one this week? Great. I don't know where anything is, they don't seem to care about cleanliness, and I don't know a soul. Thanks for all that, by the way."

"We aim to please. Hey, I'm on an important—"

"Shut up, Oriscoe. Listen, these Drow from the warehouse raid...there's something off."

Leery turned and re-entered the squad room. He passed the phone to Dru. "It's Hendrix. Speaker-phone-ify it."

Dru pressed a button and set the phone down on her desk. "Hello, Liz."

"Princess. These Drow are abnormal."

"Well, yeah. They're Drow."

"No, I mean they're abnormal *for Drow,* Oriscoe."

"What do you mean, Liz?" asked Dru.

"For one thing, their average height is about a foot short for the race. And that figure is from the 18th century, so I'd say these bodies are all a bit over a foot too short to be modern Drow."

"Well, maybe they moved to a realm that has no headroom."

Liz scoffed. "And then there's the Christmas smell."

"Christmas smell?"

"Yeah. Cinnamon. Cloves. Reindeer."

"Uh. Where are you going with all this, Hendrix?"

"There's one analogy in the history books."

"What's that?"

"The speciation of Christmas Elves from wood elf stock."

"You mean these are Christmas Drow? That seems like an oxymoron."

"Doesn't it just?" said Liz. "But there you have it. Anyway, the Icelandic have a tradition—Yule Lads, they're called. They sneak around, steal stuff, make people's lives miserable by making them move to three different labs in one week. Sound familiar?"

"Maybe a little," said Leery.

"Liz, what caused speciation of the Christmas Elves?" asked Dru.

"Directed genetic manipulation by Saint Nick. He wanted specific characteristics— loyalty, resistance to extreme cold, increased magical ability, distaste for sugar cookies and milk. Like that."

"I see. And do you think these Drow have undergone—"

"Obviously, Oriscoe. Oh, I don't know about the sugar cookies, but from what you've said about their ability to teleport, I'd say the magic augmentation is there."

"Okay," said Dru. "Anything else that might help us track them down?"

"Yeah, look for a cold environment. I'm pretty sure all this gray fur is their adaptation to subzero temperatures. Also, low light. The big eyes, you see."

"Okay. Thanks for the update, Liz," said Dru.

"No problem, Princess. When you get a chance—"

"I know. Hit him."

"You got it."

Dru tapped the disconnect and handed the phone back to Leery. "Don't worry," she said in a sultry voice. "I've found something more fun than hitting you."

33

They lined up behind the SWAT teams, lining the side of the subway tunnel. A hundred yards ahead, the tunnel branched—to the right, the Q train ran east, but the branch veering slightly left was a disused tunnel that led to an abandoned terminal near 66th Street in Central Park. Dru had dug up records of periodic deliveries of massive quantities of refrigerants—the heaviest deliveries scheduled for the summer months—all ordered by one K. Kringle.

The werewolf leading the SWAT column lifted her fist, then extended two fingers and waved them toward the MTA barricades that blocked the left-hand branch about as well as a colander held water. Servitor warriors appeared next to the barricades and began to carefully dismantle them in silence.

Once the barricade was down, the werewolf's fist pumped twice in the air, and the column began to advance at a slow walk. When she reached the leading edge of the tunnel, the werewolf peered around the corner, her ears twitching this way and that. She lifted her fist again, then dropped it, and the column of police officers surged into the dark maw of the tunnel.

Leery paced easily beside Dru, who had dressed in the tactical garb of the SWAT teams. Behind them followed fifty of the best officers the Twenty-seventh Precinct had to offer.

When the column crossed a line one hundred and fifty yards out from the disused terminal, an alarm started to shriek ahead.

"Go, go, go!" cried the werewolf commander, and everyone began to sprint toward the platform.

Dim red light bathed the platform, which seemed empty, but the light revealed a veritable army of Christmas Drow lining the tracks. With a high-pitched cry, the Drow surged forward, shaking weapons in the air and screeching their little hearts out. The SWAT officers waded into their midst, swinging claws or clubs or magical artifacts, but the Drow not actively engaged merely teleported behind them and came at the regular officers.

The Drow advanced in a lurching pace—running a few steps, pausing, teleporting, running again—and soon the well-ordered lines of the police disintegrated into chaos. Leery and Dru stood back to back, assessing the battle, trying to find the pattern of it. Four Drow popped into existence within reach of their short arms and latched onto the detectives using one hand for each.

A pop sounded, and Leery felt his arms jerk as when he'd tried waterskiing as a younger man, then his ears filled with pressure and popped. After a heartbeat of darkness, they emerged in a frigid forest hunched under a quilt of gray clouds that ran from horizon to horizon, an arctic wind blasting at them through the trunks, peppering them with ice crystals and graupel through the boughs. The Drow laughed and popped away, leaving Dru and Leery squinting at each other in the gloaming and hunching their shoulders against the wind. Dru created a pale blue rune set, activated it, and flung it above their heads. It settled toward the ground, encapsulating them in a dome of warm air.

Turning their backs on the storm, they saw a massive white structure, hazed by the effects of the snowstorm until it looked almost soft. Leery took the lead, bulling his way through the drifts—first upright, then dropping to all fours after a few steps. He bounded toward the winter palace, as Dru walked behind him, spinning a crimson rune set into existence.

Massive slabs of ice slid open, and a tall figure strode out to meet them. He wore his long, gunmetal gray hair pulled back in a loose tail behind his head, and the wind swirled it around his face, where it mingled with his long gray beard. He wore a blood-red coat that hung to mid-thigh, emblazoned with decorative gold-threaded embroidery around the white brocade cuffs and along the break line. Around his shoulders, partially obscuring the wide, white brocade collar, he wore the skin of a gray and white wolf, the jawless skull serving him as a pauldron, the tied paws hanging down his chest on the other side. Underneath the coat, he wore a fancy vest the color of arterial blood and a gold cummerbund. His ears rose to sharp points, and his eyes glowed an evil mustard yellow from dark eye sockets. Sallow white skin hung from his skull and hands, spotted with weeping sores. Silver double-bladed axes hung loosely in each hand. He stopped when he felt their scrutiny, glowering down on Leery and lifting his gloved hand to point at the wolf with a silvery ax.

"You!" he shouted. "I can see your heart, wolf! Your lusts!"

Leery made the chuffing yips that served for werewolf laughter.

"And you brought that...that *half-breed* who ruined my spell, who let LaSalle's lifeforce escape! You *cost* me, wolf!" He opened his fang-filled mouth wide and let loose a shriek that could have woken the dead. He hefted the ax in his right hand, and weak winter sunlight glinted on the runes emblazoned on its face. He charged forward, high midnight black leather boots polished to a mirror shine pumped up and down through the clean white snow, flinging a mist of crystals into the air with each step.

With a ragged snarl, Leery bounded forward to meet him. A body-length away, he leaped, becoming a brown-furred bullet aimed at Kris Kringle's throat. At the same moment, Dru empowered her rune set, and a beam of crimson light danced across the snow.

Kris Kringle flicked the ax he held in his left hand at the streak of red and the air condensed in its path, crystalizing, solidifying into a sheet of thick ice. Half-a-heartbeat later, he brought the right-hand ax whistling down into Leery's path, and thunder crackled in the snow-heavy sky.

Dru screamed, but there was nothing she could do. The silver ax batted Leery into the snow at Kringle's feet, a plume of ice and snowflakes erupting into the air on his impact—and some of them were as red as Kringle's coat. Her spell licked the wall of ice Kringle had created with a negligent flick of his hand, and the air filled with steam and the sound of a bladesmith's quench. When the steam flash-froze in the algid air and fell tinkling to the snow below, the ice wall remained—untouched—and Dru's beam of light was gone.

"Did you think it would be different?" grated Father Frost. "Did you think you could challenge me in my domain, and it would be *easy?*"

Dru's face became a rictus of anger, her eyes glowing fierce scarlet, as she began two new rune sets, both the color of gore with lines as black as death to connect them. At the same time, she chanted in the *Lingua Tenebris Lacuna,* spitting the words, biting them, puking them into the air. The already miserable gray sky darkened, black thunderheads rolling in from the horizons as she worked her magic, combining the runes and her innate magic into a hammer of wrath.

Kringle threw back his head and laughed. "My little princess, how you've grown!"

Jagged orange-red lightning stabbed down at him from the sky, but before they could touch him, he was gone, standing twenty feet away, near the trees. The bolts slammed into the ground where he'd driven Leery with his ax blow, but the only sound was the sizzle of a greased griddle as the snow and ice evaporated under the sustained the fifty-thousand-degree arc of electricity.

In a wink, Kringle disappeared from the tree line and reappeared behind her, close enough that she could smell his fetid breath, could feel the tickle of his beard dancing in the wind. Dru lunged forward, but his cold hand slapped out, still holding his ax, barring her escape with silver. He pulled her to him, and she shivered against the dreadful cold wafting off him— colder than the wind, colder than the graupel, colder than the snow and ice.

A snarling beast erupted from under the thigh-deep snow to her left, Leery vaulting from the tunnel he'd dug, his green-gold eyes blazing, his mouth wide, fangs out and ready to sink into Kringle's icy bicep. The force of his leap spun Father Frost in a half-circle, and Dru lunged out of his maniacal grip.

Kringle shook Leery loose with a mighty shrug, then lifted both axes above his head, his gaze locked on the werewolf. He lunged forward like a fencer lunging at his opponent and brought the axes whistling downward in gleaming, deadly arcs.

Leery darted away, spraying the snow with his blood from the first encounter, howling out of instinct, calling for packmates to come to his aid. Dru finished one of her rune sets, and with a scarlet flourish, flung it spinning into Kringle's face. He reared back, but the spell crashed into his face and exploded like a hand grenade staggering him, driving him back, back, back until he overbalanced and fell to the white spread of snow.

Dru grunted and began an electric blue rune set with her free hand. Her feet came up out of the deep snow, and she arched her back as bolts of pure orange power lanced down at her from the sky. Her eyes blazed brighter as the power struck, her hair floated around her in a static nimbus, and her voice grew to match the thunder rolling from horizon to horizon.

Kringle twisted over, then pushed himself upright on his knees, but before he could stand, Leery smashed into him from behind, his growl almost a physical assault in its own right. He crouched on Father Winter's back and, like a striking snake, slammed his fangs into the back of Kringle's neck. As he penetrated the man's skin, he whimpered and yipped as if Kringle's blood were acid or poison, but he didn't let go.

With a roar, Kringle threw Leery off and rolled away. He leaped to his feet, eyes dancing with ire, gaze zipping about looking for the wolf.

Dru finished her scarlet rune set and her hateful, spidery chant in the *Lingua Tenebris Lacuna,* hurling the runes at Kringle. As soon as the seventeen-pointed star left her hand, it began to grow, to morph, and flame danced along the black geometry that connected it.

Kringle made the same flicking motion as before, and another wall of thick ice appeared in the path of her spell, but Dru only grinned. Her rune set came apart, each rune spinning faster and faster, casting off rays of scarlet, dripping crimson flames. The midnight black lines that had connected the rune set tumbled end over end like telephone poles in a tornado, growing with each revolution, seeming to draw light from the red runes, from the dark sky, from the glow of her eyes, from the world itself, sucking the light away, hiding it, remaking it as darkness.

Kris Kringle began to chant, and the sound of it was like death, like pain and torture, but Dru smiled at the first syllable. She began chanting, a reflection of his chant, counterpoint in tone, inflection, even the words sounded backward to what he chanted.

He grimaced, a fierce scowl, eyes narrowed at her as the ground beneath them began to shake and shudder.

Leery raced in from behind Kringle, hunched over at the waist, snout held low so that it dug a channel through the snow as he bounded forward. He sank his fangs into the back of Kringle's thigh, just above the lich's knee, then straightened, hoping to pitch him forward into the snow. Though Kringle stopped his infernal chant to cry out, he didn't fall as Leery had hoped. Instead, Leery came away with a chunk of dead flesh in his mouth. Twisting at the waist, Father Frost swept his off-hand ax in a flat, waist-high arc, and Leery had to dance back, spitting out the gray, wormy flesh.

Thunder rolled from the blackening sky as Dru called down fire-toned lightning. The lances of eldritch plasma caught Kringle, arcing to strike the double-bladed ax he swung, and his whole body convulsed for a moment, a massive clonic seizure that made him dance and jitter. The silver ax became super-heated, the blades flashing orange and steaming in the cold air. As the lightning petered out, Kringle staggered to one knee, flinging the hot ax into the snow.

Leery had already flung himself at the Winter King's back, but Kringle sensed him getting close. He disappeared and reappeared standing behind Dru in a single heartbeat, and Leery snapped his jaws shut on empty air.

Kringle lifted his remaining ax, his murderous gaze burning down at the back of Dru's head, his brows angled down in the center, the skin of his nose wrinkled, fangs bared. He swung, putting all his strength behind the blow.

Leery fast-changed, seeming to burst from his wolf skin, born into the frigid cold as naked as a babe. "*Gregory!*" he shouted with all his essence behind it.

The magma demon appeared next to him for a nanosecond, then reappeared next to Dru, grabbed her, and disappeared them both. Kringle's full-strength swing whistled through empty space, and he shrieked with rage, glowering at Leery even as Gregory and Dru reappeared a hundred yards away.

Father Winter lifted his remaining ax and charged, not impeded by the snow in any way. In fact, he seemed propelled by it. Leery fast-changed again, his wolf bursting forth snarling, already leaping to meet Kringle's charge. The ax swept in a cold arc to meet him—a blow that would have split his skull if Gregory had left him there to take the strike.

Kringle screamed as Gregory and Leery blinked away from the path of his ax, fury sweeping out of him in a wave as cold as the space between the stars. He pirouetted, spotted Dru, and began another too-fast charge.

Leery appeared next to Dru, and half-a-nanosecond later, the massive lava demon appeared in Kringle's path, feet planted to the ground as if grown from bedrock, half-turned at the waist, leading shoulder already dropped, muscles bunched, arm held in tight to his ribs.

Father Frost slammed into him with the resounding boom of stone cracking during a quake. The impact sent Kringle staggering back, arms pinwheeling, and Gregory vanished only to appear behind him, already throwing a massive punch. The blow bent Kringle forward at the waist, and then he, too, vanished. A heartbeat passed, then he reappeared standing over his fallen ax. He swept it up in his left hand, glanced at its heat-deformed shape, and vanished again. Gregory followed suit.

Leery whirled in a full circle, gaze sweeping the landscape, trying to judge where the lich would reappear. Dru began writing crimson runes with her right hand, acid-yellow with her left. Her thunderous voice shrieked *Lingua Tenebris Lacuna* phrases that reverberated through Leery's chest.

Kringle reappeared three paces away, eyes burning with horrible rage, but before he could even inhale, Gregory appeared, smashing his fists into Kringle's body. With a choleric cry, Father Winter slammed his silver blades into Gregory, one on each side of his neck. The partially melted blade shattered, but the other bit deep, and hot magma poured from the wound like blood in the fraction of a second before Gregory melted away with a booming cry akin to massive slabs of stone falling into the sea.

Kringle smiled then and lifted his gaze to meet Leery's. But his left hand flung the useless ax haft away and clutched his side where Gregory's fist had landed. He hefted the remaining ax and took a step.

"*WHO DARES ATTACK MY KIN?*" screeched a voice of pure and fervent outrage. Lucifer appeared standing over Dru and Leery, a matte-black giant with cracks the color of burning stone zigzagging his skin, at least twenty feet tall and growing still. His burning-coal gaze met Leery's for a moment, and he nodded his head as smoke curled around his body and hissing steam enveloped his fire-singed, black-feathered wings. Then the Prince of Power leaned down at the waist and delivered a backhand blow to Father Frost that might have knocked a planet from its axis.

Kringle cartwheeled away, plowing a deep furrow in the snow, ax arcing away in a blinding flash. The force of Lucifer's blow kept him skipping across the ground until he slammed into a tree trunk with a massive crack, leaving only splinters in his wake. Then he disappeared.

"Well, that's irritating," said Luci. He looked down at Leery and Dru. "Are you injured?"

Leery shook his head, but Dru didn't break her chanting. She started to grow, her skin darkening to the color of charcoal, crimson eyes blazing like beacons, and wings made from silky black feathers sprouted from her shoulders and trailed down until they touched her heels. Scarlet light glowed from her chanting mouth, even as her tongue split and blackened. Chrome railroad spike fangs grew from her mouth, flashing in the red glow from the back of her throat. Her horns thickened and grew to sweep back over her shining raven hair like a tiara. Within seconds, she'd grown to the height of Leery's wolf. She glanced at Lucifer and nodded once.

Gregory reappeared beside them, a massive scale of basalt covering the wound he had taken. He bowed low before Dru. "My princess!" he cried. "Her Majesty, your royal mother will be so proud."

"Indeed," said Lucifer with a wide grin. "Our little princess has grown into her full power at last."

A booming roar sounded from within the mass of ice and snow. Moments later, a flood of Drow came pouring out of the gates, followed by Kringle, rearmed with a silver, rune-etched halberd.

"It seems Father Frost wants a war," said Lucifer in a mild voice. "Gregory?"

"Instantly, Your Highness." Gregory blinked out of existence, only to materialize twenty yards away at the head of one of the Eighteen Legions.

With a peal of thunder, a vicious black tear ripped through reality, and viscous black smoke came pouring through it. Almost instantly, the smoke began to take the form of a beautiful woman with elfin features and such an expression of rage distorting them that Leery felt the urge to run and hide. Agrat bat Mahlat stepped away from the rent between Gehenna and the snowy realm where they stood, and Hercule DuSang charged forth, arrayed from head to toe in plate armor wrought from fine steel and treated with hot black oxide. Gold edged each plate, with gold fleur-de-lis decorating his pauldrons. A black velvet cloak hung from his shoulders. He carried a black-bladed bastard sword, with a long pommel drawn and shaped to look like a vampire in a long black cloak. He raised his visor and gazed up at Dru with pride shining in his eyes, then saluted Leery with his sword. Then he joined Agrat standing to the side, and the rest of the Eighteen Legions poured through the tear in space and time.

Lucifer threw back his head and cried in a basso voice that shook the air, *"Belial, Beleth, Beelzebub! Attend me! Paimon, Baal, Asmodai! To me! Zagan, Purson, Gusion! Bring your legions!"*

Thunder crashed, and the ground shook as the charcoal-skinned archdemons began to materialize nearby. Legion after legion of demons came pouring out of Agrat's portal. Soon, the frozen wood brimmed with demons of all kinds—some flying, some crawling on multiple sets of limbs, some running on two legs.

And then Father Frost and his minions were upon them. The Drow struck like rattlesnakes—driving silver blades into demonic flesh, then teleporting away. Gregory and his legion of transdimensionals repaid them in kind, but when they struck, Drow disappeared and did not come back.

Lucifer's archdemons waded through the sea of twisted Drow, swinging great two-handed swords like scythes through wheat, leaving limbs, heads, and broken bodies spinning through the air in their wake.

Leery and Dru charged into the melee, ignoring the Drow if they could, dispatching them quickly if they couldn't, gazes ever settling on Kris Kringle and fighting toward him.

But the Drow kept coming from the ice palace, wave after wave of them pouring forth as though from an infinite supply.

Seeing this, Lucifer stepped forward, moving through the battle as though walking through an empty field, crushing Drow beneath his feet or kicking them aside. He bore down on Father Winter, his gaze never wavering from the creature's face.

Kringle saw him coming and dematerialized with a shouted curse. A second later, he emerged from the void between the realms and swung his halberd at Dru with a snarl.

Agrat screamed, a Valkyrie shriek of pure rage, a promise of death and destruction, and for a moment, no one moved, no one even breathed. Then she charged, dancing through the battle with the Drow, twisting, leaping, whirling around them, her burning gaze intent on Kringle, and before he could finish his swing, she was on him. She pummeled him with a flurry of five quick chops, then unloaded a roundhouse kick to his head. Kringle stumbled to the side, and Gregory was there, slamming boulder-fists into first one side, then the other, driving him back into the whirling meatgrinder that Agrat had become. With a cry, Kringle disappeared, and a heartbeat later, so did Baal and Asmodai. The trio reappeared an instant later, and in the same place. The two archdemons flung Kringle to Agrat with matching sneers.

"And thus, your treachery is repaid!" shouted Asmodai in a voice like molten bronze striking ice.

"Take your punishment, Moroz!" shouted Baal.

"You thought you could escape me, Ded?" rasped Agrat. "You're a fool!" She drove her foot into his chest, knocking him back, but again Gregory was there to herd him back with hammering blows raining down like meteor strikes.

"Sister," boomed Lucifer. "Allow me!"

Lucifer's shadow settled over the seven of them for a moment, then he reached down and grabbed Kringle in one huge hand. He shouted a word in the *Lingua Tenebris Lacuna,* and Agrat smiled as Kringle burst into flame, screeching like steam from a boiling teapot.

The Drow turned as one, then gave a mighty shout and sprinted toward Lucifer, brandishing their weapons and ignoring everyone else. Hercule slashed through their ranks, moving at a speed too fast to see anything other than a black blur, leaving great fans of blood freezing in the air in his wake.

The legions of demons cackled and jeered as they attacked the Drow from the rear.

Lucifer ignored everything but the torment of the lich named Kris Kringle—also known as Ded Moroz in Gehenna—pouring his wrath onto the screaming creature in his fist.

A few of the Drow turned and ran, flinging their weapons aside and disappearing midstride. They did not return. As Hercule and the other archdemons led Gehenna's legions to devastating effect, more and more of the Drow teleported away.

At the end, all the Drow who still drew breath abandoned Kringle, leaving the woods to the forces of Gehenna, and the trees shook with demonic cries of victory.

"My daughter," said Agrat, smiling at her. "You are beautiful!"

Dru smiled, and Kringle screamed on.

34

Lucifer pushed Kringle before him, twin manacles of shining silver binding his wrists—silver drawn from the man's own weapons and enchanted by the Lord of the Flies himself to ward against Father Frost's magic. With a wide grin that exposed his snow-white fangs, Luci ducked his cream-colored head to fit through the squad room door, and even so, his bright ginger hair brushed the top of the door frame. He turned his shoulders sideways as he stepped through, then nodded to Epatha Van Helsing. "Where would you like him, Lieutenant?"

She hooked her thumb at the holding cells behind her. "Will those manacles keep him..."

"Oh, I assure you, Lieutenant Van Helsing. He will give you no more trouble."

"Then I owe you my thanks. Again."

"No," said Lucifer. "I merely kept my word to a friend. This detestable lich was once my subject, and he stole from me...so in that sense, he is my responsibility, anyway."

"Santa is from Gehenna?"

"Ded Moroz is from Gehenna. He saw the burgeoning mythologies of this realm and left us by trickery to take up residence here."

"How..." She shook her head.

"He deceived us," said Lucifer with a stern glance at Kringle. "He seemed to die, but then returned to unlife in this realm, carrying the ability to see within an entity's heart. He lives on by sacrificing others to steal their lifeforce." He pushed Kringle into the cell and banged the door closed.

"I always knew that guy was a creep," said Leery. "Ever since I got coal that one time."

In the cell, Kris Kringle rolled his eyes and turned away.

CHAPTER 3

THE COURT CASE

I

Sam reread the indictment and frowned down at it. "If this ever gets out in the mundane world, the children will never recover." He handed the paper back to Angie. "Let's see to it this lich is locked away for centuries. Make sure this case is airtight."

Angie nodded. "It is. We don't have a confession, but with that exception, the case couldn't be stronger."

"Every time we think that..." Sam shook his head, then pinned her with his sternest gaze. "*Make sure.* Get that confession."

Angie puffed out her cheeks. "He's not talking to anyone except his magister."

"And who is that?"

"DeRothenberg."

"Of course," said Sam with a sigh. "And I bet the Dead Set will take up Kringle's cause."

"They already have," said Angie. "Marlow—the new local leader of the Set—held a press conference yesterday. He claims Kringle had a license, that the investigation, the prosecution, all of it, is an overt act of bigotry against the undead."

Sam shook his head. "A weak attempt to skew public opinion."

"An attempt to influence the jury pool."

"Yes, but we'll have our chance to do the same." He heaved another sigh. "Make sure, Angie. Triple check everything."

"I'm on it, Sam."

"And please relay my personal gratitude for His Highness's actions in bringing him in."

"Will do. Agrat and Hercule played their parts, too. And half of Gehenna if you count all the legions that came into it."

"How many were injured by this little war?"

"In the abandoned tunnel under Central Park, it got pretty grim. Twenty-three SWAT officers and thirty-seven regular officers were injured in the riot before the Drow evacuated en masse to help Kringle. In Niflhel, all the casualties were among the Drow. Leery took some lumps, but he's a tough old wolf."

"That he is. Anything from the authorities in Niflhel?"

Angie pursed her lips and shook her head. "Hel was unavailable for comment, and Loki just laughed."

"Yes, that sounds about right. Then they won't fight the prosecution here?"

Angie hitched one shoulder skyward. "There's no telling. Loki might get into it just because he's bored."

"Then let's hope he finds something on Netflix that draws his attention." Sam flashed her a little grin. "Maybe he'll binge watch that new *Loki* series from Marvel I keep hearing about."

Angie shook her head. "It's not out yet."

"Well, I'm sure he can find something. Maybe we should gift him a subscription."

"It would make a great Christmas present."

"Do you think Loki follows the tradition?"

"A Yule present, then."

Sam grinned. "Set it up."

2

Angie stood at her accustomed place in Judge Cotton Mather's courtroom. Kris Kringle stood at the defense table, silver manacles dragging at his wrists, shoulders stooped, head down. Beside him, Jeffery DeRothenberg stood with a curl to his lip and disdain in his eye.

Mather's bailiff, Robert Boyle, stood with his back to the bench, directing a stern glower back and forth across the gallery. He began to flicker as the audience continued their whispered conversations and shuffling about. He made a throat-clearing noise again—his fourth attempt to quiet the onlookers.

"Shut up or get out!" Angie cried above the din.

Boyle's gaze flicked to hers for a moment, and though she thought she saw disapproval in his, he gave her an appreciative nod as the room quieted. "Now that I have your attention," said Boyle in an utterly flat tone, "allow me to instruct you on proper comportment inside a court of law. First, there is no talking once you enter this room. His

Honor, Judge Cotton Mather, is most serious about reverence and proper respect for the Court. Flaunt his wrath at your own risk. Second, when I stand thus, you *will* give me your attention"—he swept his hand toward Angie—"Ms. Carmichael may not always be present. Third, there will be no excited utterances during the arraignments that follow. I recognize you might have a family member, or other loved one, involved in a proceeding, and that your preferred results may not be forthcoming, but I caution you. Carry on at your own risk. Recall my previous statement about Judge Mather's view as to the court. Does everyone understand?" He floated his gaze across the gallery, then nodded once. "In that case, all rise! Rise and give your respect to the judge, His Honor Cotton Mather! I call this court to order!"

As the last syllable rang through the silent courtroom, Judge Mather entered, a grave expression on his face. He hovered up to the bench and folded himself into the straight-backed wooden chair there. He lay his spectral hand on his gavel and cleared his throat. Then he picked up the gavel and gave his sound block a solid thump. "Be seated," he said. "Robert, what is the first matter before us?"

"The arraignment of one Kris Kringle, also known as Dagmar Kerstman, Einar Julenissen, Ded Moroz, Nicholas Sinter, Martin Kristkind, Othidn Vetramathur, Den Che Lao Ren, Hoteiosho Kurosho, and Yol Tomta."

Mather lifted an eyebrow, then shifted his gaze to Kringle. "My, you've been busy, haven't you? And, if I might add, by all appearances, up to no good."

"Your Honor," droned DeRothenberg, "if I may make a motion before we proceed?"

Mather sniffed and narrowed his eyes. "Most irregular, sir. We shall not have difficulties, shall we?"

DeRothenberg forced a smile on his face. "No, Your Honor. It's only that this arraignment is an utter waste of the Court's valuable time. You see, my client—"

"Mr. DeRothenberg! I don't recall acceding to your request." Mather shifted his gaze to Robert Boyle. "Robert, did I grant this magister leave to present his motion and somehow forget the act?"

"No, Your Honor," said Boyle, glowering at DeRothenberg.

The magister spread his hands and bowed his head. "I humbly beg your forgiveness, Judge Mather. I meant no disrespect. I am eager to represent my client is all."

Cotton harumphed, then made a show of adjusting papers, his gavel, the sound block, and anything else he could find on his desktop. "In future, sir, I would caution you to pay more attention to my person while arguing in this courtroom."

"Yes, Your Honor. Again, I apologize."

"Yes, well..." Mather glanced at Angie, a quick nip, then away again. "Now, using succinct language, tell me of this utter waste of time."

DeRothenberg smiled and lifted his head. "Yes, Your Honor. As you may know, Judge Mather, my client was...ahem...captured in the realm of Niflhel. I—"

"No, I am not aware, but neither does it matter."

The vampire magister tucked his chin toward his chest. "Your Honor, I believe it may, begging your pardon. You see, my client is the de facto sovereign of Niflhel. As such—"

"Your Honor! This is ridiculous. This lich is no more the ruler of Niflhel than he is a cheery old man who loves children. This is baseless—"

"Madame Prosecutor, if I may interrupt? You speak out of turn. If you intend to present an objection, it is not properly formed. If you do not, I would offer you the same advice I recently offered your opponent."

"Sorry, Your Honor," said Angie. "May I try again?"

Mather nodded once. "Please do."

"Your Honor, I object to Mr. DeRothenberg's characterization of events. In addition, I challenge his assertion that Kris Kringle is the ruler of Niflhel. According to the fifth edition of *Realm Royalty*, Niflhel is ruled by Her Majesty, Queen Hel."

Cotton smiled. "Nicely done, Madam Prosecutor."

"Thank you, Judge Mather."

Mather turned to DeRothenberg. "Your response, sir?"

"Thank you, Your Honor. The fifth edition of *Realm Royalty* notwithstanding, Queen Hel has neglected Niflhel for centuries. In effect, she is an absentee sovereign, and my client, Kris Kringle, has taken up the mantle, the responsibilities, and the leadership of the realm. I've an affidavit—"

"Let's wait a moment," said Mather, patting the air at DeRothenberg. "Let's slow down, shall we? First, whether your client—and I would call him by name, but I'm afraid I don't know which one to use—has assisted the rightful queen of Niflhel or not makes little difference. You see, according to Canon and Covenants, the current edition of *Realm Royalty* is the authority on the sovereignty of each of the Nine Realms. The current edition, I might add, is the fifth edition. As such, I cannot recognize your client as the sovereign of Niflhel."

"But, Your Honor, if I may—"

"Sir, I have made my ruling. And in any case, this is more appropriately a matter for the trial judge. I encourage you to take it up with him or her." He turned his gaze to Angie. "Do the People have a position on bail?"

"You bet, Your Honor," she said with a pretty grin. "The accused is indicted for two counts of kidnapping, two counts of attempted magical murder of a law enforcement officer, resisting arrest with violence and maleficia, incitement to riot, and off-license harvesting resulting in true-death. As the charges indicate, the accused has already performed many serious acts of defiance against the lawfully appointed officers of the Court in this jurisdiction, and since that includes fleeing the realm itself, the People request remand."

"Preposterous, Your Honor," said DeRothenberg. "My client is a property owner, a business owner, with many ties to the community. Further, His Majesty Lucifer of Gehenna has *unlawfully* applied enchantments on my client." He grabbed Kringle's wrist and rattled the manacles' chain. "He did this in the realm of Niflhel, then transported my client here against his will. We will bring charges against His Majesty—"

"Again, all this about His Majesty is irrelevant, even if true. As to your other arguments, owning property, businesses, etc., I find them less than compelling in light of your client's actions."

"Then, Judge Mather, may I point out that these *alleged* actions of my client have not been proven? How can we use the crimes he is accused of to prove bail should be denied during the trial on those crimes?"

"Allow me to demonstrate the method," said Mather in a droll voice. He picked up his gavel. "The accused, Kris Kringle or by any of his numerous aliases, is remanded to the custody of the Locus of New York's Department of Corrections and bound over for trial on a short date." He banged the gavel. "Next case, Robert."

3

Sam stood in the lobby and applauded as Angie walked in. She grinned and waved her clasped hands over first one shoulder, then the next. "I got him held over for trial, but even better, DeRothenberg tipped his hand."

Sam arched an eyebrow.

"He's going to argue the Covenant of Outrealm Sovereign Immunity applies to Kringle. He tried it with Judge Mather during the arraignment."

"Ah. He had to know Mather would deny that motion on its face. He's far from stupid. Maybe it was a feint."

"Perhaps," Angie said with a shrug, "but I didn't get that feeling. Plus, Mather gave him hope. He encouraged him to argue the motion in front of the trial judge."

Sam nodded. "I hope he does. The fifth edition—"

"That's what I used in my counterargument, and Mather made it clear the book was the basis of the law. I bet DeRothenberg attacks that point."

"When was the fifth edition released?"

"1991," said Angie with a frown.

Sam nodded. "We'd better prepare a strong argument on that point."

"I'm on it."

4

Seated at the prosecution table, Sam craned his neck to look behind them. Judge Crowley's courtroom bristled beyond capacity by the trial's start time, with the overflow standing along the back wall of the gallery. Bailiff Haddo frowned at the low-level susurration, then called the session to order.

Aleister Crowley materialized on the bench, sat, then focused on his gavel. With a groan of effort, he picked it up and bounced it off the sound block. "Be seated." He glanced up at the people standing in the back. "If you have a seat, that is. I warn you all in advance: no foolishness." He turned his attention to Sam. "Are the people prepared with an opening statement?"

Jeffery DeRothenberg stood, cleared his throat, and said, "Your Honor? There is a matter we must address before opening statements. The resolution of the matter might obviate the need for openings."

Crowley's lips flattened. "Yes, Cotton said you might have a motion. Generally speaking, Mr. DeRothenberg, I prefer that pretrial motions happen *before* the trial begins."

DeRothenberg smiled and nodded. "Exactly why I brought it up now, Your Honor."

Crowley puffed out his cheeks but nodded. "Proceed."

"Thank you, Your Honor. Let me eschew formality and get straight to the heart of things. My client, Kris Kringle, is the de facto sovereign of Niflhel. As such—"

"Your Honor, if I may?"

"Yes, Ms. Carmichael?

Angie got to her feet and flashed a fake smile at DeRothenberg. "Your Honor, in the interest of not wasting the Court's time, Judge Mather has already ruled on this matter."

"Is that true, Mr. DeRothenberg?" asked Crowley.

"I do not agree with that assessment, Your Honor. Judge Mather ruled that the argument could not be used in arraignment but encouraged me to present the argument in this venue. He went so far as to rule that the motion is more appropriately dealt with here."

Crowley glanced at Sam, then gazed up at the rafters. Finally, he lowered his gaze and said, "I will hear the argument."

DeRothenberg treated Angie to a gloating smile, then turned back to the bench. "Thank you, Judge Crowley." He glanced down at Kris Kringle, then lay a hand on his shoulder. "You see, my client has performed the duties of a sovereign, taken the responsibility for the realm, acted to maintain it, and, in essence, has taken the *abandoned* throne of Niflhel."

Crowley lifted an eyebrow. "And what does Queen Hel have to say about that?"

"The former queen is silent on this matter— as she is on all matters, Judge."

"I see. I assume this is leading to the Covenant of Out-realm Sovereign Immunity?"

DeRothenberg nodded. "It is, Your Honor."

"Are you not aware, sir, that the covenant provides an explicit definition as to who may be considered a sovereign under the law?"

"I am, Your Honor." He picked up a brand-new copy of *Realm Royalty.* "I'd like to offer this as evidence."

Crowley nodded.

DeRothenberg smiled and approached the bench. He lay the book on the desktop, then flipped it open to the front matter. "Your Honor, I refer you to the date of publication for this volume."

Crowley peered down at the tiny print. "This is the fifth edition, published in 1991."

"Yes, Your Honor. I would submit that as nearly thirty years have elapsed since its printing, this edition is insufficient for the covenant's purposes."

"Your Honor, the Locus Magister's Office has spoken to the publisher of *Realm Royalty,* and I believe their response to our questions speaks to this point," said Sam as he got to his feet.

"Do we really need witnesses and such?" asked Crowley, perhaps a bit peevishly.

"No, Judge Crowley. I have a written statement—"

"Your Honor, I must object," said DeRothenberg. "Am I to take the provenance of this statement as—"

"Yes, Mr. DeRothenberg," said Crowley. "I will admit the statement as evidence for the purposes of this motion."

"Thank you, Your Honor," said Sam. He approached the bench and lay the multi-page statement in front of the judge. "I have taken the liberty of summarizing the statement on the first page."

"Many thanks, many thanks," murmured Crowley. His translucent eyes flicked back and forth in his immaterial eye sockets as he read the entire statement—twice. "Yes, I see." He raised his gaze to DeRothenberg's face. "Sir, the publisher of this book admits the fifth edition was published twenty-nine years ago but has updated it with each printing—the latest of which occurred three years ago." The judge turned to Sam. "Would you be so kind as to find the page on Niflhel?"

"Certainly, Your Honor." Sam fanned through the pages, watching the page numbers. He stopped about two-thirds of the way through the thick volume. "Here it is."

Crowley's gaze flicked back and forth once more as he read, signaling Sam with a nod when he wanted the page turned. Finally, he grunted. "As I suspected, Mr. DeRothenberg. Your client is not even mentioned among the nobles of Niflhel."

"But, Your Honor, my client does everything for the realm, while Queen Hel does nothing. He maintains the populace, he performs civic duties, directs the constabulary—what there is of it—in fact, he performs all the executive functions while taking no payment, receiving no rewards for his service. He does so, simply because the queen shirks her responsibilities, abandoning the society, the culture, and the realm itself to decay and ruin. Surely, the actions of a sovereign are more important than the ink used to print that book."

Crowley spread his hands. "Not according to the law, sir. I am a judge, not a legislator. If you'd like the Covenant changed, I suggest you address someone who is the latter. In the meantime, the trial will proceed."

DeRothenberg frowned. "Then I request permission to present the argument to the jury as an affirmative defense."

McCoy frowned down at his feet. "Your Honor, I have no idea how that would work."

"Nor I, Mr. Prosecutor."

The old vampire magister grunted, then said, "It's simple when you give it some thought. My client believes *he* is the rightful sovereign of Niflhel. As such, when the police officers began nosing around his...food source, shall we say? As the police disrupted his only method of sustaining his life, he took it as an attack on his royal person. In other words, he viewed it as an act of war."

"Preposterous, Your Honor," said Sam. "First of all, what Mr. Kringle believes is irrelevant to the matter. And, since he is not the rightful ruler of Niflhel, his person is not royal. Further, no action taken by the police could reasonably be construed as an attack."

DeRothenberg shrugged. "Naturally, Mr. McCoy doesn't recognize the bigotry in his statement since he does not rely on the essence of others to maintain his life, but the prejudice against the undead inherent in his statement speaks volumes."

Sam turned his head to stare at DeRothenberg, his mouth slightly agape.

Crowley held up a hand. "Can we not, Mr. DeRothenberg? Can we not descend into the petty name-calling, the finger-pointing?"

The vampire shrugged. "It is what it is, Your Honor. The police removed my client's feeding charms—the enchantments he relied on to bind the essences of his cattle to the maintenance of his existence." He waved it all away. "But let's ignore that. My client disputes the charge of off-license harvesting leading to true-death, but is willing to plead that matter out, if Your Honor insists, so long as the other charges are dismissed."

Crowley exhaled with a loud sound somewhere between a growl and a groan and shook his head. "Mr. DeRothenberg, that hardly seems a good-faith offer."

"Nor a reasonable one, Your Honor," added McCoy.

"Fine. Let us dispense with that charge and proceed with an affirmative defense on the other charges. Allow the jury to decide whether my client's actions were reasonable."

Crowley leaned back, drifting halfway through the chair back before catching himself and stiffening his immaterial spine. He scratched his chin, gazed up at the rafters, then blew out another breath with the same harsh sound. He spent a few moments staring at the vampire magister, then at the lich sitting at the defense table, then finally, glanced at Sam. "No, Mr. DeRothenberg, I think not. What we will do is proceed with all the charges, but I will allow you to plead your affirmative defense for the charges of resisting arrest with violence and maleficia, plus the incitement to riot charge."

"But the kidnapping and attempted magical murder charges go part and parcel with the resisting arrest charges. Surely, Your Honor, what fits one set of crimes must also fit all like crimes?"

Crowley shook his head. "I disagree, sir. It is a reasonable act to resist what may legitimately be perceived as an unlawful attack on one's person, but that does *not* extend to forcible kidnapping or murder in some other realm to which one has escaped."

DeRothenberg looked down at his shoes for a moment. "Very well, Your Honor. In light of that, I must move to have the charges of kidnapping vacated, as my client wasn't present. Lesser beings who serve—"

"Kringle used Drow he personally mutated to suit his will in order to perform the kidnappings, Your Honor," said McCoy. "He can hardly claim to have no hand in it."

"These 'mutated' creatures, as Mr. McCoy calls them, are defined by their loyal natures, Your Honor. When *they* perceived a threat to my client, *they* acted to eliminate that threat. Without my client's knowledge or direction, Your Honor. We can call witnesses to testify to that fact."

Crowley turned to McCoy and arched one eyebrow.

Sam shook his head. "By Mr. DeRothenberg's own admission, the nature of these witnesses is defined by their fanatical loyalty to the defendant. Surely, if they are willing to kidnap police officers in his name, lying won't be much of a stretch."

"The truthfulness of witness testimony is a matter for the jury, Your Honor," said DeRothenberg.

"Not if their truthful testimony is impossible, Your Honor. The defendant *genetically modified* these Drow. He bred them for ultimate loyalty."

Crowley lifted his chin. "It strikes me that there is an easy solution. Mr. McCoy, would the People be satisfied if we amend the kidnapping charge to a conspiracy count? Sentencing would fall under my purview."

McCoy looked up at the ghostly judge for the space of a few breaths. "Yes, Your Honor, I believe I could accept that."

"Very well. Mr. DeRothenberg—"

"Excuse me, Your Honor," said the vampire. "But I find myself compelled to move that you recuse yourself from this trial."

"Wuh-what?" sputtered Crowley.

DeRothenberg shrugged and gave him a sheepish look. "Your relationship with the royal family of Gehenna is well known, Judge Crowley. In light of that, and coupled with the agreement you just struck with Mr. McCoy, it has become plain that your impartiality cannot be trusted."

"We struck no agreement, sir," said Crowley in a voice as cold as winter in Niflhel. "I find your implication distasteful in the extreme."

"Then how can I rely on impartial rulings?"

"Be careful, sir! Be careful!" snapped Crowley. "As to your motion that I recuse myself, it is denied with extreme prejudice. The charges of kidnapping stand, and I'll advise the prosecutor to add charges of conspiracy to kidnap."

McCoy nodded his agreement.

"We will proceed, then. You may present an affirmative defense to the resisting and incitement charges only. Have I made myself clear?"

DeRothenberg frowned and narrowed his eyes to furious slits, but he nodded, nonetheless.

"Good. Step back." As the two magisters returned to their tables, Crowley concentrated on picking up the statement from the publishers of *Realm Royalty,* slipping it inside the front cover of the book, then signaling Sam to remove the book. "Mr. Prosecutor, are you ready to proceed with your opening statement?"

"I am, Your Honor."

"Very well. Bailiff Haddo, fetch our jurors."

"Thank you, Judge Crowley." Sam came around to face the jury box as Haddo brought them in, smiling like a grandfather with a pocketful of candy. Once they had taken their seats, Sam stepped closer. "Ladies and gentlemen of the jury, my name is Sam McCoy. I'm the Executive Assistant Locus Magister.

My job is to prosecute individuals who commit crimes in this locus. In other words, my job is to present evidence of criminal wrongdoing to jurors like yourselves. Some cases are more difficult than others, of course, depending on the strength of that evidence." He spun on his heel and looked at the defense table. "This is not one of those difficult cases. It all starts with the lich seated at the defense table—a creature who has used many names to hide his identity. That, in itself, makes his innocence seem less likely, doesn't it? I will present evidence over the course of this trial that the lich now known as Kris Kringle is, in fact, an ice demon named Ded Moroz. He even uses that name as one of his many aliases." Sam pointed at Kringle. "Take a good look, ladies and gentlemen, but do not be fooled by the fancy costume. Look deeper. Examine his skin, his eyes, note his unfriendly expression. Is this the Santa Claus of popular myth?" Sam shook his head. "Kringle is a lich. He maintains his existence by stealing the lifeforce—the essence—of his victims. The Canon and Covenants provide for his existence through something known as the Covenant of Improper Action. The CIA is the basis for the hunting licenses some of you may have. No doubt, we all understand that each license bears restrictions. The defendant ignored the restrictions that bound his license, and instead, he took such sustenance as was convenient. Further, he took *more* sustenance than was allowable under the terms of his license. We call these criminal acts off-license harvesting, and in this case, his harvesting has led to the true-death of his victims. Again, true-death is allowable under the Covenant of Improper Action when the creature's specific needs require it. That is not the case in this matter." He turned and walked back to the prosecution table. "Multiple burial sites were discovered in Central Park. Numerous staked vampires were discovered buried head down, numerous elves were found in a mass grave, and my compatriots on the Covenancy Magister's Office for the Southern District tell me there is every indication that there are more mass graves, more racially segregated collections of remains likely to be found during their very detailed examination of the park. Further, each victim found so far was enchanted and their lifeforce redirected to the defendant's use. We know this because he *signed* the enchantments, believing, I must assume, that no one would be able to decipher his runes." McCoy smiled. "But the police employ one of the Nephilim, and you will hear directly from him as to the nature of the enchantments." Sam put his hands behind his back and strode back to stand in front of the jury foreman. "Those crimes—the off-license harvesting leading to true-death—are at the heart of this matter. The discovery of the bodies led to the police investigation. As the police got closer and closer to discovering the defendant's identity, he set his minions to lay in ambush at one location, then to overwhelm the police force in another. Further, he sent a small group of these minions to kidnap two police officers and deliver them to the defendant's home in the realm of Niflhel. Once he had them there, he set about trying to kill them using the magic at his disposal and silver weapons. Failing in his attempt, he went on to resist arrest with violence and maleficia." Sam tucked his chin to his chest and made a show of bending down to rest his palms on the rail of the jury box. "You will hear from an August Person who, despite the Covenant of Sovereign Privilege, has volunteered his time and testimony to help put this vile actor away. You will also hear from highly decorated police officers, including one of the officers kidnapped by the defendant." He turned and looked coldly at DeRothenberg. "My colleague, Jeffery DeRothenberg, represents the defendant. He is his magister, and his job, no matter how distasteful you might find it, is to zealously attempt to convince you that Mr. Kringle should walk free." Sam turned back to the jurors. "How will he do that? I imagine he will present a defense claiming Mr. Kringle thought of himself as the sovereign of Niflhel—which is patently untrue. He will blur the intent of the Covenant of Out-realm Sovereign Immunity, trying to turn it into an affirmative defense, trying to make you believe the police officers acted improperly, that it was reasonable for Kringle to believe their attempts to enforce the Canon and Covenants was an attack from our realm against Niflhel. Nothing could be further from the truth, and during this trial, I will prove that. I encourage you to always keep two points in mind. First, all of the crimes stem from the defendant's off-license harvesting leading to true-death. Second, the defendant's actions—the hiding of his identity, the laying of ambushes, of kidnapping police officers and whisking them away to another realm—imply the defendant's knowledge of guilt. In other, plainer words, the defendant knew what he was doing was wrong, and he acted to protect himself from prosecution for his crimes. Innocent entities don't do that. Innocent entities cooperate to clear their names. Innocent entities do not try to murder the police trying to find them." Sam turned and pointed to Kringle. "This entity did attempt to murder two police officers, no matter what excuse he gives for it." He walked back to the prosecution table. "Thank you for your attention, ladies and gentlemen of the jury. Thank you, Your Honor. I'm finished."

Crowley nodded and extended an empty hand at DeRothenberg, who stood, jerked his vest straight, glanced at Sam, then strode to the center of the courtroom.

"Hello, ladies and gentlemen. I am Jeffery DeRothenberg, a magister and a vampire. For Mr. McCoy, issues revolving around licensing are academic. Pure. A matter of the letter of the law. Those of us who live in the real world, who must hunt for our sustenance, know the reality of these laws." He shook his head, looking at each juror sadly. "Off-license harvesting? If only life fit into clearly defined boxes. Licenses bound by restrictions, taking what prey was convenient, taking more than necessary…" Again, DeRothenberg shook his head. "Spoken by a man with more food in his refrigerator than he needs, who eats his fill—and likely more—at every meal, whose only dietary restrictions are imposed by how much he's willing to spend at Le Cirque." He turned and glared at McCoy a moment. "I should find his statements on the matter offensive, but to be honest, I'm simply too tired of fighting prejudice like this." He threw his arms wide. "We claim to be an enlightened society. We have covenants such as the Covenant of Improper Action to protect those poor fools who must hunt to eat. We have covenants such as the Covenant of Competition to help those poor unfortunates who have trouble eating because of all the damn restrictions written into their hunting licenses by people like Mr. McCoy—unfeeling people who have never dealt with true hunger in their lives." DeRothenberg sighed as though the weight of the world rested on his shoulders. "McCoy says the so-called off-license harvesting leading to true-death lies at the heart of this case, but if you'll pardon my speech, that's pure poppycock. Governmental overreach lies at the center of this mess. McCoy, and men like him, lie at the center of this charade because they are the ones who set up the situation that made this case possible."

Sam shook his head and rolled his eyes.

"Yes, McCoy, show me your disdain. I'd rather have it out in the open than hidden by that cultivated veneer of acceptance, of magnanimity, of your hand extended to help." He turned back to the jurors with a crisp snap of his heels. "Those of you on the jury who are de facto second-class citizens as I am, know all too well that I'm speaking the truth."

Judge Crowley cleared his throat.

DeRothenberg nodded. "Message received, Your Honor." He nodded to the vampire juror, to the lich, the wight, and the silkie. "We know all these truths, anyway. Restating them isn't necessary. So...back to McCoy's arguments. First, my client was not aware his actions were considered off-license—and we dispute they are, by the way. Second, my client was unaware of any investigation into his actions. No one from the police, the LM's office, or anyone else contacted my client. He had no knowledge that the Magical Examiner exhumed and interfered with his cattle. In fact, he had no idea that the werewolf and demon who invaded his lands in the realm of Niflhel were police officers from the Locus of New York. They did not identify themselves. They served no warrants, and they made no calls to me, Mr. Kringle's magister. They just showed up in battle fatigues and wolf-skin. My client naturally assumed his royal person was under attack—"

Judge Crowley again cleared his throat.

DeRothenberg held up a hand. "There is dispute about the royal status of my client. Another *legal* nitpick. However, that doesn't change the fact that my client *believed* in his own sovereignty. The ruler of record for Niflhel, Queen Hel, has not ruled the realm in fact for centuries. She makes no decrees, maintains no public lands, allows no audiences. Niflhel is, in fact, abandoned, and my client stepped up and began serving the people of his realm. He took up the maintenance of public lands, nurtured the culture, the society there. He served as the chief executive, and he did it all out of a sense of duty. That's right"—DeRothenberg nodded emphatically and struck his palm with his fist—"this lich of whom Mr. McCoy paints such an evil picture, performed the role of the sovereign of Niflhel for no reward, no recompense, no recognition. Only because he felt it was the *right thing to do.*" DeRothenberg whirled in dramatic fashion and pointed at Kringle. "My client is *that* kind of entity—one who is concerned with the betterment of his people, not one with this so-called knowledge of guilt that McCoy prattled on about." Again, his gaze swept the vampire, the lich, the wight, and the silkie. "*We* know how things were in previous centuries. We *lived* with the prejudice against those of our kind. Aliases indicating knowledge of guilt! The immortal among us remember having to change names, to 'inherit' our assets just to avoid persecution. We remember!" He turned a gelid gaze on Sam. "Knowledge of guilt? Perhaps you are correct, Mr. McCoy, but the guilt in question is not my client's! No, the guilt belongs to men like you. Men who made our lives so horrible, who made us live in fear of a stake in the chest, of a head-down burial, of sudden decapitation as we slept the days away. Is it any wonder my client's first assumption on seeing two strangers arrayed for battle and advancing toward his house was that they were there to attack him?" His gaze zipped to the silkie's. "Is it so strange?" He turned to the wight. "So unbelievable?" He met the vampire's frank gaze. "So impossible he might have been right?" His gaze came to rest on the lich. "Haven't we all thought the same thing at least once? No, McCoy doesn't understand. He doesn't believe that thought is reasonable." He pivoted on his heels and, with his arms tucked behind his back, glared at Sam. "*He is wrong!*" DeRothenberg held his pose for a few silent moments, then walked to his chair and sat down.

"Am I to take it you've finished?" asked Aleister.

"Yes, Judge," said the vampire magister.

Angie leaned close to Sam and whispered, "Jury nullification? That speech hurt us."

Sam nodded.

"Mr. McCoy? Are you ready to call your first witness?"

"Yes, Your Honor. The People call Hercule DuSang."

People in the gallery gasped, and a murmuring roar grew as Aleister pounded his gavel on his sound block. Bailiff Haddo headed toward the witness room door and slid through it without opening it. After a moment, after the audience had quieted, the door opened and

Haddo led Hercule, dressed in a crushed black velvet cloak with a red lining, a tuxedo made from shimmering dark gray pashmina over a crisp white shirt, a matching red silk bow tie and cummerbund, into the courtroom. He led the vampire through the oath, then seated him in the witness box.

Through it all, Sam sat behind the prosecution table, staring at nothing, seemingly lost in thought. He stood and approached the witness box without looking up. "Hello, Your Royal Highness," said Sam.

"Hello, again, Mr. McCoy. I wish our meeting were under better circumstances."

"As do I, sir. As do I. Sir, pardon my bluntness, but you are a vampire of some...uh..."

"Tenure?" offered Hercule with a smile. "Yes, Mr. McCoy. I am old. Some might call me ancient." He turned and winked at the vampire in the jury box.

"Would you be so kind as to list your aliases?"

Hercule lifted a shoulder and let it drop. "I have none."

Sam turned and glanced at DeRothenberg. "Opposing counsel seems to believe every immortal undead has a string of them. Have you had to hide from government agents? From men such as myself?"

Hercule treated him to a kind smile. "No, Mr. McCoy. Werewolves during the War of Fangs, yes. Misguided paladins, yes. Government agents? No."

"I see. And why didn't you need aliases? Why didn't you live in fear of...how did Mr. DeRothenberg put it? Oh, yes. Why didn't you live in fear of a stake in the chest?"

"Well, I must admit that for a time, I did. Mostly from the paladins, long before the Covenancy was formed."

"How did you avoid needing aliases?"

"*Je suis né dans la noblesse d'épée.* Born as a Noble of the Sword, yes? An aristocrat. My family's holdings were rich. After I inherited at the untimely death of my father, at the time of my own change, I was able to close the gates of my castle and live within unmolested. The clients—peasants and merchants alike—I supported came to know of my new life, but, due to the long patronage of my family and despite the edicts of the church, they never came to believe I was evil. Just...*different.* In fact, many in the village petitioned to extend our relationship, to strengthen the bond to my family, through the Ritual of Blood."

"You mean conversion to vampirekind?"

"*D'accord.*"

"I see. Then there was a way to avoid all the deceit, to live in peace with the mundanes surrounding you?"

"Yes," said Hercule with a glance at DeRothenberg. "Through *respect* and mutual understanding—something this fool knows little about."

"Pardon, Your Royal Highness," said Judge Crowley. "But please refrain from—"

"My apologies, Aleister—uh, Your Honor."

"Thank you, sir."

"Mr. DuSang, did you have occasion to travel to Niflhel recently?"

"*Oui.* My daughter and her partner were there."

"Your royal daughter, Drusilla bat Agrat, known in this realm as Detective Dru Nogan?"

"*Oui,* and her partner, Leery Oriscoe." He turned to the jury. "Though not of noble blood, he is a fine werewolf of impeccable honor." When the vampire juror sneered, Hercule narrowed his eyes at him. "*Non! Non, monsieur!* Do not disrespect him in my presence!"

"Sir," said Crowley. "Please."

"*Oui, Juge* Crowley. Your pardon. But I will hear no disrespect of Leery Oriscoe."

"So noted," said Aleister. "Let us hope everyone in attendance notes it as well."

Sam lay one hand on the bar of the witness box. "Mr. DuSang, why were Detectives Nogan and Oriscoe in Niflhel?"

"At the moment I was called to assist them, I didn't know. Gregory, our driver, teleported home at the command of my royal brother-in-law, His Majesty, Lucifer ben Mahlat." Hercule's hand fluttered toward his jugular. "Gregory, himself, had taken a wound. He informed us of the danger to Drus—to the detectives. My wife and I were obliged to make the journey."

"And your wife is Her Royal Majesty, Agrat bat Mahlat, Sovereign of Demons, Commander of the Eighteen Legions, Queen of the Shabbat, Angel of Divine and Sacred Prostitution, Dancing Roof-Demon, Mistress of Sorcery, One of the Four Queens of Gehenna, She of the Great and Terrible Name?"

Hercule smiled. "*Oui*, though I don't find her name so terrible." A chuckle ran through the room, and Hercule smiled wider.

"What did you find on your arrival?"

Hercule sobered, turned his head, and glowered at Kringle. "*Que enculé—*"

Judge Crowley coughed, then cleared his throat.

"*Je m'excuse*, Aleister. *Je m'excuse.* When Agrat and I arrived, that…*traitre* sitting at the defense table *portant des armes de guerre* coming toward my daughter and Leery. Preceding him, an army of deformed Drow threatened my daughter, as well."

"Sounds ugly," said McCoy.

"*Oui, moche, affreux, horrible.*" Hercule stared daggers at Kringle. "I regret circumstance did not allow me to *parler avec ce crétin de l'honneur et de la bonne conduit!*"

Kringle's eyes blazed a baleful yellow, then narrowed to slits.

"*Oui? Oui, salaud? Vous souhaitez dire quelque chose? Je m'en réjouis! Nommez l'heure et le lieu!*" Hercule came half out of his seat, eyes blazing, hand groping for the sword that did not hang on his hip.

Sam lay a hand on his elbow and stepped into his line of sight. "Please, sir."

"Yes," said Hercule, cheeks pink with fury. "I forget myself. I apologize yet again. *Je m'excuse*, Aleister. *Je m'excuse,* Mr. McCoy. *Je m'excuse, mesdames et messieurs du jury.*"

"Your Honor," said DeRothenberg with a sigh. "Must we endure more of this?"

Hercule turned and glowered at him. "Shall we, too, meet for a discussion?"

DeRothenberg rolled his eyes and held his hands out toward the judge.

"Sir, please try to control your anger," said Aleister, turning his gaze on Hercule. "Your *understandable* anger." He looked at DeRothenberg and narrowed his eyes. "Overruled."

DeRothenberg rolled his eyes and sighed.

McCoy stepped between the defense table and Hercule. He smiled and gave the old vampire an encouraging nod. "My French isn't that great, so please pardon me if I misunderstood."

Hercule nodded graciously.

"After the defendant came carrying weapons of war, after the ugly, frightful, horrible scene of the Drow and the defendant advancing on your daughter and her partner, what happened?"

Hercule gave a brisk nod. "My lovely wife, Gregory, my royal brother-in-law, and some of his lieutenants—"

"The archdemons Baal and Asmodai?"

Hercule nodded. "Yes, and Dru and Leery. They took Ded Moroz in hand and began his...*education*. It fell to me, numerous legions of Gehenna, and several other archdemons to deal with the *déformé* Drow."

"In the interest of clarity, when you say Ded Moroz, you are referring to the defendant."

"Yes. Once, he was nothing more than a rather annoying ice demon by that name."

"Do you know how he came to live in Niflhel?"

"*Oui,* but Lucifer knows more of the specifics."

"Very well," said McCoy. "What happened after you dealt with the distorted Drow?"

Hercule shrugged and smiled. "Close, *Monsieur,* but I said, 'deformed.' Anyway, after we dealt with them, and after Lucifer finished...*speaking* to the defendant, he fashioned a set of silver manacles from the arms *le crétin* carried, then enchanted them to block the defendant's magic." He leaned out to look. "The same manacles he still wears. Then, my brother-in-law delivered the defendant to the police in this fine locus."

"Thank you, sir," said Sam.

"*C'est mon plaisir et mon devoir.* No thanks are necessary."

"Well, you have them, nonetheless."

Hercule inclined his head.

Sam turned and returned to the prosecution table. "No more questions for this witness at this time, Your Honor."

"Very well, Mr. McCoy." He turned a stern look on the defense table. "Mr. DeRothenberg, would you like to question this witness?"

"Oh, indeed I would!" He sprang to his feet and moved toward the witness box.

"Then allow me to set some ground rules, Mr. DeRothenberg," said Aleister in a deceptively mild voice. "Rule one: I will tolerate no disrespect of this witness. Rule two: you will not seek to enrage His Royal Highness. Rule three: break these rules at your own risk."

DeRothenberg scoffed and rolled his eyes.

"Not an auspicious start, sir," grated Judge Crowley.

"My apologies, Your Honor," said DeRothenberg in the most insincere voice imaginable. "May I at least do my job? May I at least cross-examine this obviously prosecution-friendly witness?"

Crowley narrowed his eyes and stared down at the vampire magister. "Sir," he said in a soft voice. "You begin to try my patience. Perhaps writing me a check for five hundred dollars will help you remember your place."

DeRothenberg flapped a hand and turned his gaze on Hercule. "DuSang—"

"A thousand, then?" asked the judge.

DeRothenberg took a long, slow breath, eyes closed. When he opened them again, his expression had softened. "Your Royal Highness," he said and bowed his head. "Did I hear you correctly? You have never had to hide behind a false identity?"

"That is correct," said Hercule in a bored tone. "I have sworn it, no?"

"Oh, yes, that's right. You are part of the royal family of Gehenna, aren't you? You married into it?"

"*D'accord.* Everyone knows this."

"And when did you join the family? When did you meet Agrat bat Mahlat?"

"The answers to those questions differ. I met Agrat toward the end of the War. We married ten years later."

"I see. Do you recall the year of your marriage?"

"Of course. 1497."

"So, to restate the testimony you gave Mr. McCoy, before the War of Fangs, you lived in relative bliss with a village full of adoring clients who did not believe—as everyone else at the time did—that you were in league with Satan?"

Hercule shrugged. "I don't like your language—*ce qui ne me surprend pas vu le peu que je t'aime*—but, in essence, you are correct."

DeRothenberg grinned, then winked at the undead in the jury. "Ah. Does it strike you as odd, sir, that when you wish to speak disrespectfully, *tu parles français?*"

Hercule scoffed. "*Incorrect, imbécile.* I speak my native tongue when I'm upset or excited. I am perfectly able to give idiots like you the proper respect in any language."

Nodding, the defense magister chuckled to himself. "So it seems, sir. But returning to my question, after the War, you carried on in your bucolic bliss for ten whole years before leaving the realm for your wife's palace in Gehenna?"

Hercule yawned. "Yes, yes. What of it?"

"Well, to those of us who weren't born as Nobles of the Sword, those of us without the privileged birth of French aristocrats, it is clear why you never used aliases, why you didn't encounter little men like Mr. McCoy. *You. Weren't. Here.*"

Hercule rolled his eyes. "*Et maintenant viennent les plaintes de la paysannerie...* DeRothenberg"—Hercule allowed a sly grin to split his face—"or should we use your *real name*?"

The vampire magister scoffed and narrowed his eyes. "I'll have you know that Jeffrey DeRothenberg is my real name."

Hercule burst into laughter. "No, it isn't, *Ulrich Bauer*. Do you find it ironic to be named thus? A first name meaning rich noble and a surname meaning beggar? What happened? Did your family lose all it had?"

DeRothenberg turned away. "I'm asking the questions."

"*Sir!*" snapped Hercule.

"Sir," grated DeRothenberg. "What did you do during the War of Fangs? *Sir.*"

Hercule sniffed. "I did what we all did."

"That's not very specific. I'd like to know—"

"Your Honor," said Sam, rising to his feet. "I fear this is not the time to assuage Mr. DeRothenberg's itch for ancient history."

Aleister Crowley nodded. "Sustained. Move on, Mr. DeRothenberg."

"Is it not true that you commanded—"

"Your Honor!" cried McCoy.

"—*an assassination squad?* One that didn't much care whether its victims were wolf or mundane? That you *feasted* on the blood of your—"

"Mr. DeRothenberg!" snapped Crowley. "That, sir, will cost you *five* thousand dollars. You may return to your seat if you have no *relevant* question for this witness."

DeRothenberg closed his eyes, breathing heavily, hands clenched. "A few more questions, Your Honor." Without opening his eyes, he turned toward the jury box. "What did Lucifer—"

"*His Royal Majesty!*" snapped Hercule.

"As you wish. What did His Royal Majesty, Lucifer, King of Gehenna, do to my client?"

"Do? I've already said."

"No, sir. You alluded to him speaking to my client, educating him. Did he touch my client? Did he *burn* my client?"

Hercule leaned back, a sneer on his face. "I was *engaged*. It was very much like a war—"

"Ah! Then you admit your time in Niflhel was like an invasion?"

"I did not say that."

"'Very much like a war,' I believe you said."

"*Oui*. Not because of what *we* did. Because of what your client's minions did. The number of them, the teleporting, the silver weapons."

"And your legions of demons came unarmed? Perhaps bearing handfuls of flowers? You went dressed as you are now?"

"No, of course not. I went dressed to defend my daughter and my very good friend, Leery Oriscoe, from the deformed denizens of your client's house. I wore my armor from the War. I carried my sword. I went prepared to kill whoever threatened my family."

"You went prepared for war?"

"Yes."

"You went to kill my client?"

"No."

"You traveled to Niflhel to help your daughter assassinate my client, just as you assassinated thousands during the War of Fangs! Admit it!"

Hercule laughed, long and loud. "No, poor Ulrich. I went to Niflhel because your client tried to kill those under my sworn protection. I went because your client, wielding silver weapons, attacked my *daughter.* I went to *defend,* not to assassinate."

DeRothenberg turned without another word and walked to his seat. "Nothing else." He sank to his seat, pink blotches high on his cheeks, gaze burning on the center of his table.

"Very well," said Judge Crowley. "Thank you, Your Royal Highness."

"My pleasure, *mon très cher ami.*" Hercule rose, and as he did, he turned a narrow-eyed glare at the defense table. He pinned both DeRothenberg and Kringle with a glower as he walked past, then continued down the aisle through the gallery and out the door.

"Your next witness, Mr. McCoy?"

"Thank you, Your Honor. The People call Detective Sergeant Leery Oriscoe of the NYPD's Supernatural Inquisitors Squad."

Leery was fetched, sworn in, and sat in the witness box, and through it all, his face bore his characteristic grin. Sam approached him with an answering grin. "Hello, Detective Oriscoe."

"Hello, Mr. McCoy. Nice day for a trial."

"It is," said Sam. "Will you please tell the jury how you became involved in this case?"

"Sure. Basically, I'm a cop, and cops get called when a civilian stumbles over a dead foot sticking up through the snow in the North Woods section of Central Park."

With a wry smile, Sam shook his head. "Is it going to be that kind of direct, Detective?"

"Oh," said Leery through a big grin, "I'm afraid it is." He winked at the jury.

"Very well. We'll muddle through the sarcasm."

"You'll try, you mean," said Leery.

Sam grinned and shook his head. "Please tell us how you began the investigation."

"Sure. It all started with some dead vampires." He glanced at the jury. "And by dead, I mean really dead. They'd been staked with enchanted stakes, then buried head down with the soles of their feet left exposed to the sky."

"Why would someone go to all that trouble?"

Leery shrugged. "From what I'm given to understand, the paladins developed this method of dispatching a vampire back in the Middle Ages. They thought the head-down orientation would confuse a vampire if the stake happened to come loose."

DeRothenberg scoffed.

Sam glanced at him over his shoulder, then turned back to Leery. "I see. Were those remains exhumed and examined by the ME?"

"Sure," said Leery. "I had them all sent to Liz Hendrix because she's the best. But let's keep that last bit just between us. I don't want to give her the big head."

"I'll see what I can do, Detective. What did Dr. Hendrix discover?"

"That the stakes were enchanted using a mix of Enochian runes and a language she couldn't identify."

"Ah. Was that obstacle overcome?"

"Yeah. My pal from the Maleficium Cryptogenia Unit, Vinny Gonofrio, is one of the Nephilim. He came down to the ME's and read the other runes. He said they came from a language called Proto-Elamite and that the enchantments did two things: enchant the lifeforce of the victim and bind it to the enchanter's use, and make it hard to remove the stakes."

"I see. Were the stakes eventually removed?"

"Vinny got one of them out. He had to make a special request, though." Leery pointed at the ceiling.

"I assume you mean he invoked Heavenly power?"

"Yeah. Once he did that, the spike popped right out, and the victim subsequently turned to dust."

"Were you able to identify the victim before that happened?"

"Oh, definitely. I knew him, you see. He was a bigoted bloodsucker named Antoine LaSalle." Leery turned his gaze on DeRothenberg. "It's amazing, but Mr. DeRothenberg was his magister as well."

"Yes, Mr. DeRothenberg's client list is very interesting," said Sam. "And were you able to learn anything else from the runes?"

Leery nodded and glanced at Kringle. "Yeah, the idiot signed it. Yoltomta."

"Strange name," said Sam.

"Yeah. From what Detective Gonofrio said, it's Old Norse, and it means 'Christmas elf.' We later learned it was two names, Yol Tomta. Christmas, well, Yule, I suppose, and Elf."

"How did you discover that?"

"Detective Gonofrio again. He did some genealogical research. An entity name Yol Tomta immigrated here in 1608. He also found a string of suspicious inheritances."

"What made them suspicious?" Sam turned to the jury and put his hands behind his back.

"All of the names were part of the Santa Claus mythos in one form or another."

"Ah. Do you recall the names?"

Leery nodded and pulled out his notes. "Yol Tomta, Einar Julenissen, Nicholas Sinter, Othidn Vetramathur, Martin Kristkind, Dagmar Kerstman, Ded Moroz, Dun Che Lao Ren, and Hoteiosho Kurosho. All of those are references to the names for Santa Claus or a similar figure in different mundane cultures."

"I see. Besides the inheritance records, did you come across this set of names in another way?"

"We did," said Leery with a nod for the jury. "The bodies of the vampires had been stolen from the ME's office by a team of what we learned were mutated Drow." Leery paused while the audience gasped and carried on. "At about the same time, we'd come across more bodies in the park—this time elves. We put them in a backup location, but Liz Hendrix also affixed magical trackers to the remains, expecting these Christmas Drow to come after them as well."

"Christmas Drow?"

Leery grinned. "I know it sounds ridiculous. Bear with me a moment, and I'll explain."

Sam nodded.

"We tracked the elvish remains to the warehouse of Kerstman Industries. At that time, we hadn't spoken to Detective Gonofrio yet, so the name didn't mean anything to us. My partner and I were part of the second wave. We found a hallway of executive offices. Each one bore one of the names Detective Gonofrio turned up in the inheritance records."

"I see. An interesting coincidence."

"Uh, sure."

"And what happened in that warehouse, Detective?"

"The Christmas Drow had set an ambush, but we took care of them."

"And?"

"Well, when Dr. Hendrix examined the remains—"

"Were there no survivors?"

"Plenty, but they could teleport, and we weren't prepared with wards, so..."

"So, the living escaped."

Leery nodded. "Anyway, Dr. Hendrix examined the remains and determined they had been genetically modified in a manner similar to Christmas Elves."

"Ah. Christmas Drow, I see," said Sam, and Leery nodded. "Did you learn anything else?"

"We traced Dagmar Kerstman to his apartment but were told he had passed away—which we found suspicious."

"How did you come to investigate the defendant?"

"Well, he's all of them. Yol Tomta, Sinter, Kristkind, Kerstman, et cetera. They are all aliases of the lich seated at the defense table."

"And how did you come across his Kris Kringle identity?"

"When we couldn't find out who would inherit from Kerstman, we decided to try other names associated with Santa Claus that hadn't been used yet. Kris Kringle seemed obvious, so we started there."

"I see."

"And we also looked for locations in the locus that were suitable for the mutated Drow."

"And did you find anything like that?"

"Yes, an abandoned subway terminal under Central Park. We found many deliveries of refrigerants there, all ordered by a K. Kringle."

"Then what happened?"

"We set up a massive raid with the SWAT units and a gaggle of officers from the Two-Seven."

"The Twenty-seventh Precinct? Your precinct?"

"Yes, to both questions."

"How did the raid go?"

"As we approached the terminal's platform from the subway tunnels, we were attacked by an army of Christmas Drow."

"An army?"

Leery shrugged. "That's how it seemed at the time. There were a lot of them, and they came at us in formation and with a specific strategy."

"I see. And up to this point, what crimes were you investigating?"

"Well, we had the bodies, improperly disposed of. At that point, we didn't know if we had a serial killer on our hands or a sloppy licensee. Of course, there were the robberies by the Drow—stealing the bodies, I mean—so I guess we could add theft and interfering with an official investigation. Really, we just needed to speak to Kringle."

"I see. And what happened when this army of genetically-manipulated Drow encountered your force of SWAT and regular officers?"

"They began fighting—they had silver melee weapons."

"And how was the fighting resolved?"

"I don't know. Remember how I said they had a strategy?"

"Yes."

"It was to kidnap my partner and me. Well, perhaps that was a tactic, and they definitely had other tactics, but the point is, Detective Nogan and I were surrounded by four of the little buggers, and they teleported us to the middle of a frozen forest. Now, I know it was in Niflhel, but at the time, neither of us had a clue to where we'd been transported."

"Did you have any means to return?"

"No, not immediately." Leery thought for a moment. "Actually, I think I just misspoke. We could have called on a transdimensional demon named Gregory. He's part of the household of my partner's parents, and I've been granted the right to call on him when we need help. My partner definitely has that right, but neither of us thought of it before Kringle attacked us."

"So, to recount your testimony, you were transported against your will to an unknown realm, left in the middle of a frozen forest, and before you had a chance to gather your wits, the defendant attacked you?"

"That's about the size of it."

Sam nodded, then met the gaze of each juror in turn. "And you are sure, beyond any hint of doubt, that the defendant is the one who attacked you?"

"Absolutely. Since I'm a werewolf, the fight got up close and personal. I sank my fangs into his flesh many times."

"And I assume he threatened your life?"

"Many times," said Leery gravely. "He wielded two double-bladed axes forged from silver. He also threatened my partner's life on multiple occasions."

"I'm glad he wasn't able to make good his threats."

"Me, too, Counselor," said Leery with a chuckle.

"So, up until you were kidnapped and forced into a confrontation with the defendant, the charges you had against him were relatively small?"

"That's about the size of it. Had he shown us his ticket and cooperated, I'm sure that, though he might have gotten in a little trouble given the fact he ignored the stipulations of his license and didn't dispose of the remains properly, he wouldn't be sitting here facing the charges he is now."

Sam nodded. "How was this unplanned and unwanted trip to Niflhel concluded?"

Leery nodded and turned to the jury. "My partner and I were unable to bring the attack to an end, and at one point, the defendant revealed he had the power to teleport much as his Drow did. He teleported behind my partner and swung his ax in what would have been a killing blow. I was too far away to stop it, so I fast-changed and called Gregory's name. He appeared and rescued Detective Nogan."

"And how did the defendant react to that development?" asked Sam, half-turning toward the defense table to look at Kringle.

"With rage. He attacked Gregory using his teleportation and his axes. Gregory was eventually injured—a cut to his neck—and he returned to Gehenna."

"And that's when certain individuals from your partner's home realm joined the fight?"

Leery nodded. "Gregory brought Lucifer ben Mahlat, Agrat bat Mahlat, Hercule DuSang, and the Eighteen Legions."

Sam lifted his eyebrows. "An intimidating retinue. The king, one of the queens, the prince, and eighteen of the finest legions of demon-warriors the realm has to offer. How did the defendant respond?"

"With another army of Drow."

"I see. What happened next?"

"Seeing the numbers coming at him, His Majesty Lucifer called nine of his archdemons. I think they were Belial, Beelzebub, Beleth, Paimon, Baal, Asmodai, Zagan, Purson, and Gusion. Some of them brought their personal commands—about a bajillion screaming demons. We began to battle the Drow, but when the defendant threatened my partner, Gregory, Her Majesty, Baal, Asmodai, and His Majesty took issue. The defendant was detained while the rest of the forces from Gehenna mopped up his army of Drow."

"And, subsequently, the defendant was delivered to the custody of the NYPD at the Twenty-seventh Precinct?"

"That's right," said Leery. "And there he sits." He pointed at Kringle.

"Very well. Thank you, Detective."

"Any time, Mr. McCoy."

Sam turned and looked at Judge Crowley. "That's all I have for this witness, Your Honor."

Crowley nodded once. "Mr. DeRothenberg?"

With a grimace of distaste, the defense magister rose and approached the witness stand. "Detective Oriscoe, is it?"

"You know good and well it is," said Leery with a bright smile.

"Let's take a moment and review parts of your testimony, shall we?"

"That is what I'm here for."

"You mentioned that another policeman removed my client's charm from one of the bodies?"

"Yeah, Detective Gonofrio."

"Were you aware of the damage that act would do to my client?"

"Pal, we didn't even know who your client was at that point."

"But you knew the stake was enchanted in the manner of lich?"

"Not until we removed it."

"And why not?"

"Gonofrio couldn't read the full enchantment."

"Oh?"

Leery flashed a lopsided smile at the jury. "Well, the stake was embedded in a vampire's chest, and it resisted ordinary methods of removing it. So, yeah, we had to pull it to read the parts hidden by LaSalle's flesh."

DeRothenberg frowned and cast a surreptitious glance at the vampire on the jury. "Then once you removed it, you grew concerned that you may have caused harm to my client?"

"Again, we didn't know your client was even involved."

"How can that be? You learned his name during the process, correct?"

"Not really. You see, your client went to great lengths to keep his actions hidden."

"How so?"

"He wrote in a dead language that almost no one could have identified. He put his name down at the tip of the stake where we had to remove it to read it. He used a name from antiquity. He had his minions steal the bodies rather than allow us to continue our investigations when he could have merely contacted the police. Those seem like the acts of a guilty conscience to me."

DeRothenberg snapped his head around to address Crowley. "Your Honor, I demand the last response be stricken from the record. It is non-responsive."

"No, Mr. DeRothenberg. You did ask."

The magister grimaced and dropped his gaze to the floor. "Detective, how many Drow did you and your partner murder in my client's warehouse?"

"None," said Leery as his expression hardened.

"Then how did the ME have bodies to examine? Were they murdered by other officers?"

"No Drow were murdered during the raid. They attacked my partner and me with weapons crafted to be deadly to us and in great numbers. We applied what force was necessary to defend ourselves."

"After you forced your way into the warehouse?"

"We conducted a legal raid backed by a search warrant."

"So, during your so-called legal raid backed by a search warrant, you took the lives of how many Drow?"

"As many as forced us in the defense of our own lives."

"And how many, *exactly,* is that?"

"I don't know," said Leery. "I didn't count them, and to be honest, I don't particularly *want* to know the count."

"Why not? Are you not proud of your actions?"

"Did I kill them? Yes. Would I kill them again? Yes, all things being equal, and in the defense of Dru's life or my own. Did I enjoy it? Take pride in it? No. I'd rather they'd given up or, better yet, left us alone entirely."

DeRothenberg scoffed. "The werewolves I knew during the War of the Fangs—"

"Are irrelevant to this discussion," said Leery.

The vampire glowered down at him through a pinched gaze. "You said you identified my client via sales records for refrigerants. Why did you not approach my client directly and ask for an explanation?"

"We did. He responded by sending an army of Drow against us, by kidnapping—"

"No! You launched an all-out attack on that subway terminal!"

"—my partner and me, then by attacking us personally."

"Fine, yes. Let's discuss this so-called personal attack. When you appeared unannounced, uninvited on my client's Niflhel estate, did you identify yourselves as police officers?"

"Appeared? Unannounced? Uninvited?" Leery scoffed. "Your client *had us kidnapped,* Counselor. He *knew* who we were. That's kind of the point of kidnapping, isn't it?"

"You say you were kidnapped, and maybe you were, but not by my client!"

"By his minions, from a place your client owns to another place your client owns."

"But my client took no part in it. Unless you've left out salient facts. And, you haven't answered my question. Did you identify yourselves?"

"My partner was wearing a uniform."

"And *did you identify yourselves?*"

Leery glared up at him and said nothing.

"Your Honor, I ask you direct the witness to answer."

"Detective?"

Leery scoffed. "No, we didn't say our names."

"And you reacted to my client's approach with violence?"

"We reacted to your client's unprovoked, violent attack with violence, yes. But do you know what I just remembered? Your client knew who we were. He *admitted* he knew who we were."

"How convenient, but I didn't ask."

"He said he could see into my heart. He went on to say he knew I'd called Detective Gonofrio to read his runes, that Gonofrio had cost him by removing the spike from LaSalle's chest."

"Non-responsive, Your Honor! I demand that be stricken from the record!"

"Please, Mr. DeRothenberg. You opened this door. Do you have other questions for this witness?"

DeRothenberg puffed out his cheeks. "Just one, Your Honor. Oriscoe, you said His Majesty Lucifer detained my client. Isn't it true that he *tortured* my client?"

A lopsided grin surfaced on Leery's face. "Not that I saw."

"No? Was my client not burned in the king's grasp? Was he not set aflame?"

"You'd have to ask His Majesty."

"You didn't see it with your own eyes?"

"Your client had just brutally attacked me. He cut me with silver-edged weapons, struck me many blows. I'm afraid I don't recall."

"And isn't that convenient?" DeRothenberg flashed a meaningful look at the undead jury members. "I have nothing more for this witness." He stomped back to his seat.

"The witness is excused," said Crowley. "I believe we could use a break. Court will reconvene after lunch." He struck his gavel on the sound block and disappeared.

5

After lunch, Sam called for the testimony of Liz Hendrix followed by Vinny Gonofrio. Both reinforced what Leery had already testified to, and DeRothenberg gave them no more than a cursory cross. As Vinny left the courtroom, Sam stood. "Your Honor, I call the transdimensional entity known as Gregory of Gehenna."

"Very well," said Crowley, and before the sound of his words died, Gregory appeared next to the witness box. He'd come in his human shape, though a glimmer of hot magma still shone in his eyes. Bailiff Haddo swore him in and asked him to take his place in the witness box.

Sam stood and came around the prosecution table. "Thank you for coming, Gregory."

The demon nodded, then glanced at the jury. "This is my first time doing this testifying thing. Please pardon my mistakes." He gave the jury a little bow of his head.

"It's easy, Gregory," said Sam. "The only requirement is that you tell the truth."

Gregory nodded once more, and Sam turned to watch the jury.

"We've heard during previous testimony that Detective Leery Oriscoe 'called on you' during a moment of need. Is that true to your recollection?"

"Of course," said Gregory. "Leery is an honorable wolf. He doesn't spread untruths." DeRothenberg snorted, and Gregory narrowed his eyes at the magister.

"Ignore his antics," said McCoy. "His intent is to sow disbelief in the jury because he has no factual basis to impugn Detective Oriscoe's testimony."

"I...see," said Gregory.

"Can you tell us what prompted Detective Oriscoe's call for help?"

"That man"—he pointed at Kringle—"had gotten behind Princess Drusilla and was attempting to murder her."

Sam nodded. "And you were able to save her?"

"I am transdimensional. That allowed me to arrive before the blow struck and whisk the princess to safety."

"I see. And what do you surmise would have happened if Detective Oriscoe hadn't called on you?"

Gregory shrugged. "The blow would have struck Princess Drusilla. Leery did right to call on me."

"How did the defendant react?"

"With rage, sir. With rage." He turned his orange-tinted gaze to glower at Kringle. "First, he directed his rage at Leery, but I stopped him from causing additional harm to the wolf. Then, he redirected his attack toward Princess Drusilla again, and I took it upon myself to stop him."

"And you did that by?"

"I engaged him in combat," said Gregory. "Normally, my nature makes the outcome of such combat a foregone conclusion, but in this case, the defendant had a rudimentary form of my ability to be anywhere at any time. He used it to his advantage and was able to injure me slightly."

"What happened then?"

"Having recognized the defendant for who he really is, I knew I had to notify my king, and being injured anyway, I decided on a quick trip to do just that."

"You returned to Gehenna? What about the defendant's identity prompted that?"

"He is Ded Moroz, an ice demon of little renown in Gehenna, with the exception of having exchanged his demonic existence for the existence of a lich."

"Why would His Majesty be interested in that?"

"He broke laws in Gehenna. He…stole from the king. His Majesty always deals with lawbreakers in the end."

"I see. I take it you were part of the battle that followed His Majesty's arrival in Niflhel?"

Gregory nodded. "I was."

"Can you describe the battle?"

"The defendant sent little, broken creatures against us. On the whole, they were uninteresting, except they had the ability to transport themselves in the manner of my people. My liege commanded me to fetch a legion from Gehenna, and when I returned to get them, Queen Agrat and His Royal Highness, Prince Hercule, the events incensed them to great anger. They decided to come along, and the queen brought the rest of the Eighteen Legions."

"And after you returned?"

"We began to fight, but the defendant once again focused on Princess Drusilla and attempted her murder, which, of course, drew the wrath of her royal mother, myself, His Majesty, and two of His Majesty's lieutenants. The defendant did not fare well in the exchange."

"I would guess not. How did the battle end?"

"His Majesty took the defendant in hand."

"And?"

"And after the defendant's creatures were contained, we delivered the defendant to authorities in this realm."

"Very well," said Sam, nodding to the jury. "At any time, did you see either detective do anything that could be taken as an unwarranted attack on the defendant?"

Gregory shook his head. "They only defended themselves against his attacks."

"Thank you, Gregory. I have no further questions for you at this time."

Gregory nodded once more, then turned his gaze on DeRothenberg. The defense magister stood, patted Kringle on the shoulder, then came across to stand in front of Gregory. "That was quite a story," he said.

"It is what happened."

"We shall see. We shall see." DeRothenberg whirled to face the jury. "Tell the truth! *You* transported the detectives to Niflhel, didn't you?"

"No."

"You did, and you did it as part of revenge planned by His Majesty. Isn't that the case?"

"No."

"Oh, come now! You don't expect the fine people in the jury box to believe such fanciful tales, do you? That you came at the beck and call of a mere werewolf? That you happened to recognize this lich during the course of your admittedly short exposure to him?"

"That is what happened," said Gregory with a shrug. "And besides, Detective Oriscoe is a werewolf, that much is true, but he is no 'mere' werewolf. He has *earned* the right to call on me. He is a brave and honorable wolf."

"Of course he is." DeRothenberg rolled his eyes and scoffed. "How is it you recognized my client after all the intervening years?"

Gregory grinned. "I am transdimensional, sir. Time, to me, is nothing."

DeRothenberg frowned as though confused. "What features led you to believe my client was this Ded Moroz of whom you speak?"

Gregory glanced at Kringle and shrugged. "All of them. He is the spitting image of Ded Moroz, except for the lack of life."

"Then why hasn't he been found before? Why didn't the king send minions after him?"

"You'd have to ask His Majesty."

"Fine!" snapped the vampire. "Then, let's speak of how my client was abused by the king and queen of Gehenna."

"Abused?" Gregory shook his head ponderously. "He was not abused. He drew the queen's wrath, and he fought her. I came to her aid. Baal and Asmodai, as well. Any injuries he sustained are his own fault."

"And the king? How did the king treat him?"

"Appropriately, sir."

"Describe His Majesty's actions!"

Gregory turned to Aleister Crowley. "Your Honor, I've been instructed not to answer questions such as this."

"Why is that?" asked Aleister.

"They impinge on matters relating to the internal security of Gehenna, and I am not at liberty to discuss them."

"I see," said Crowley gravely. He turned his level gaze on DeRothenberg.

"Oh, come now, Your Honor! You can't possibly—"

"Move along, Mr. DeRothenberg."

"But—"

Crowley held up his hand. "Do as I bid you, sir. Have you anything else for this witness?"

"Isn't it true that His Majesty burned my—"

"I cannot answer."

DeRothenberg glared at Gregory, his fists clenched at his side. "Did my client— No, strike that. Was my client injured in the custody of His Majesty?"

"Again, I cannot answer."

"Was he burned?"

Gregory glanced at Judge Crowley.

"Mr. DeRothenberg, that is enough. I have ruled on this matter. Have you finished your cross?"

DeRothenberg snapped an angry gaze up to meet Crowley's. "Since you won't let me ask the necessary questions, I guess I have."

"Then sit down, sir!" cried Crowley, letting his frustration crackle in his voice. He glowered at the vampire magister as he returned to his seat, then took a long pause to compose himself. He turned to Gregory and said, "Thank you, sir, for coming to our realm and testifying today. You have my personal thanks. You may step down."

Gregory inclined his head and disappeared.

Sam stood, glanced at the jury, then brought his gaze up to meet Crowley's. "Your Honor, the prosecution rests."

"Very well, Mr. McCoy. Mr. DeRothenberg, might I suggest you take the rest of the afternoon to compose yourself? We can begin your case in the morning."

"No, Your Honor, I'm fine," said DeRothenberg in a steely voice. "I prefer to begin now."

"Very well," said the judge. "Call your first witness, sir."

"I call His Majesty, Lucifer ben Mahlat, King of Gehenna, Lord of the Flies, Prince of Darkness, Father of Lies, the Great Shaytan,

Day-Star, Son of The Morning, Tempter, Angel of Light, Lord of the Air, the Great Adversary, the Roaring Lion, Angel of the Abyss, the Dragon Lord, He of the Great and Terrible Name."

Sam leaped to his feet. "Your Honor!"

Crowley frowned at DeRothenberg. "This is most unusual."

"I have a right to call this witness, Your Honor. He features heavily in the case."

"That may be true, Your Honor, but the Covenant of Sovereign Privilege—"

"May not be asserted by Mr. McCoy."

"Very well," said Judge Crowley. "I will reach out to His Highness and ask if he is willing to testify."

Gregory appeared behind the bar. He handed Sam three scrolls, then disappeared. Sam unrolled the first and read it to the end. Then he peeked at the top few lines of each of the others.

"Well, Mr. McCoy?" asked Aleister.

"Your Honor, I have received, by hand-delivery, the response of His Majesty, Lucifer ben Mahlat to the question you were about to ask. His Majesty declines, quoting the Covenant of Sovereign Privilege."

Crowley flicked his gaze to DeRothenberg. "There you have it, sir."

"Then I call Her Majesty—"

"Your Honor?" asked Sam, holding up the second scroll.

"I think not, Mr. DeRothenberg."

"Of course not," muttered the vampire. "Then I must call Detective Dru Nogan."

Sam held up the third scroll. "Your Honor, Detective Nogan, as she is known in this realm, is also Princess Drusilla bat Agrat of Gehenna. She, too, asserts Sovereign Privilege."

"But she can't do that!" exclaimed DeRothenberg. "A mere princess is not a sovereign! Plus, she is a police officer!"

Crowley smiled and turned to Sam, then quirked an eyebrow.

"Princess Drusilla bat Agrat is the heir-apparent to the throne of Gehenna, Your Honor. Named as both her royal mother's heir and also the heir of her royal uncle."

"And there you have it, Mr. DeRothenberg. The Covenant of Sovereign Privilege does apply to the heir apparent. You may call her as a police officer, but you may not ask her any questions related to the governing of Gehenna.

The actions of any of the rulers of Gehenna are off-limits. Likewise, any citizen of the realm who has no legal link to this realm. Is that clear?"

DeRothenberg closed his eyes a moment. "Then I call Professor Anders Blight."

The old man was led in and helped to the stand, then sworn in and allowed to sink into the chair with obvious relief. DeRothenberg approached him with a thumping stride, making the professor rear away. "Professor, can you elucidate the Covenant of Sovereignty with Regard to Realms?"

"Well...I *can,* but it would be best if you ask me about the part you care about. It's quite long."

"Of course," said DeRothenberg. "When is it permissible for a monarch to respond in a martial manner?"

"Ah, I see." Blight peered at the jury while stroking his long white beard. "A ruler may defend against threats with military might under three main rules. First, of course, is invasion by the military of another realm. Second, when his royal person is threatened by agents of another realm. Third, and I might note that this has never happened, when the mundane population of his realm attempt to secede from the supernatural population."

"Yes, thank you," said DeRothenberg. "Can you expand on the second rule? What constitutes an agent of another realm?"

"Any person or persons linked to the official government of another realm."

"A princess—especially one who is the heir apparent—would be such a person?"

"I suppose," said Blight.

"And her lover?"

"No, I don't think so. Maybe." Anders thought for a moment, stroking his beard. "Yes, I think he would."

"Thank you. I have nothing else, Your Honor."

Crowley lifted an eyebrow. "Mr. McCoy?"

"Thank you, Your Honor. I'll keep this short." He stood but didn't come around the table. "Professor Blight, can you repeat the second rule?"

"Military response is justified when a sovereign's royal person is threatened by agents of another realm."

"Thank you. Who, exactly is the sovereign? How do we distinguish the actual person?"

"Ah, that's easy. The Canon and Covenants command us to maintain a book called *Realm Royalty,* in which we must maintain accurate records of the royal families, duly elected officials, and other sovereigns for each realm."

"Yes, of course," said Sam. "And is there any provision for, say, someone who is dissatisfied with the official monarch's job performance?"

"I'm not sure what you mean," said Anders.

"Say a person decides his lawful monarch has abandoned her realm. Can that person merely assume the role of monarch?"

Blight huffed a breath. "Certainly not! That would lead to chaos!"

McCoy picked up the copy of *Realm Royalty* and walked to the witness stand. "Professor Blight, can I impose on you to read the name of the sovereign of Niflhel?"

"Oh... I... That is..." The old man patted various places on his robe for a moment, then smiled and withdrew a pair of glasses. "That is, certainly!" He took the book from McCoy, consulted the index, then shuffled through the pages. "Ah! It says here the sovereign of Niflhel is Queen Hel herself."

McCoy nodded at the jury. "And can you read the edition number of this volume?"

Blight nodded and flipped to the front of the book. "Fifth edition."

"Thank you, Professor. Do the covenants specify that the most recent edition is the only version of this book that matters?"

"Well, that is a gross paraphrasing of the covenant, but yes, I suppose it will do."

Sam nodded and handed the professor his letter from the publishers. "Can you tell me which edition is the most recent?"

"Hmm. This is a letter from the publisher, and...yes, here it is. The most recent edition, and therefore the edition of record, is the fifth edition." He thumped his free hand on the copy of *Realm Royalty* he still held on his lap.

"Given this information, do you have an opinion on whether the defendant in this case would be justified in presenting military action against anyone?"

"Most certainly not!" said Blight, his expression a caricature of horror. "Then any person could simply amass a private, personal army and begin attacking anyone he pleased! Chaos, Mr. McCoy. Chaos!"

"Yes, I suppose it would be. Thank you, Professor Blight." McCoy took the book, opened it to the page on Niflhel, and then passed it to the juror foreman, who looked at it and passed it on. Then Sam handed over the letter, turned, smiled at Anders Blight, and took his seat. "No more questions, Your Honor."

Aleister nodded and turned to the defense table. "Have you any other witnesses, Mr. DeRothenberg?"

For several minutes, the vampire didn't look up, didn't speak, didn't move. Finally, he shook his head. "None that would change anything, Your Honor. The defense rests."

CHAPTER 4

THE VERDICT

I

The jury was out for less than an hour before alerting Judge Crowley that they'd reached a verdict. Sam and Angie rushed back down to the courthouse and ran into Leery and Dru on the steps outside. "Counselors," said Leery by way of greeting. "This is good news, right?"

"I can't imagine it has gone any other way," said Sam. "But let's go in and find out."

Judge Crowley's courtroom was filled to capacity again, and Leery and Dru found places against the back wall. Sam and Angie took their seats, and as soon as they did, Bailiff Haddo called the court to order.

Judge Aleister Crowley appeared on the bench, already seated. He grasped the gavel and rapped it on the sound block. "Be seated, ladies and gentlemen. I've called you back to dispense with the matter of the People versus Kris Kringle and all his numerous aliases." He turned to the jury foreman. "Mr. Foreman, do you have a verdict for each and every count?"

"Yes, Your Honor."

"Fine," said Crowley. "Are the verdicts unanimous?"

"They are, Your Honor."

"Then allow me to ask you your verdict on the charges of kidnapping?"

"Guilty, Your Honor."

"Then I shall waive the conspiracy charges. How say you to the charges of attempted magical murder of law enforcement officers?"

"Guilty on both counts, Judge."

"Very well. On the count of resisting arrest with violence and maleficia?"

"Guilty."

"And incitement to riot?"

"Also guilty, Your Honor."

"Lastly, then, how do you find on the nineteen counts of off-license harvesting leading to true-death?"

"All guilty, Your Honor."

DeRothenberg shot to his feet. "Poll the jury, Your Honor?"

"I can, but I fail to see the point."

"It is still my client's right to hear the jury polled, Your Honor," said DeRothenberg, staring at the lich on the jury.

"Fine. I will poll the jury as to all counts. If you cannot answer in the affirmative for all counts, I direct you to answer in the negative," said Crowley, staring at the jury. "With that understanding, Mr. Foreman, do you find the defendant guilty on all counts?"

"I do, Your Honor."

"Thank you. Juror number two, do you find the defendant guilty?"

"Yes, Your Honor."

Crowley went down the line, and each juror answered in the affirmative, even the wight, the vampire, the silkie, and the lich. As each of the undead answered, DeRothenberg's shoulders slumped a little more. As the last juror's answer rang through the courtroom, he nodded and resumed his seat.

"Very well," said Crowley. "The Court thanks you, ladies and gentlemen, for your service in this matter." He turned to the defense table. "Rise, please, so I may issue sentence." Everyone stood, and Judge Crowley nodded. "Kris Kringle, having been found guilty by a jury of your peers, it falls to me to render sentence. On the two counts of kidnapping, I sentence you to two concurrent terms of twenty-five years to a lifetime. On the two counts of attempted magical murder of a law enforcement officer, I also sentence you to concurrent sentences of twenty-five years to life, but consecutive to the kidnapping sentence. Resisting arrest with violence and maleficia bears a mandatory sentence of fifteen years, also to be served consecutively. For incitement to riot, I sentence you to sixty-three consecutive months. And now, for the nineteen counts of off-license harvesting leading to true-death, I sentence you to three months for each count, to be served *consecutively*. I make this distinction as I find myself agreeing with Detective Oriscoe and Mr. McCoy. Had you merely cooperated, I would have sentenced you to much less time, possibly even a fine, but as things are, I want you to feel it, sir. All told, your sentence in a dungeon to be determined by the Locus of New York's Department of Corrections spans, at minimum, seventy-five years. I suggest you use the time to better yourself, to seek the therapy and counseling available through the Department of Corrections that you may emerge from your time away a better entity, one who may make a positive contribution to the Covenancy." He smacked the sound block with his gavel. "So ordered. Court dismissed."

CHAPTER 5

THE END

I

After watching Santa Claus led away to serve his time, Leery and Dru left the courtroom. In the hallway outside, Leery said, "Well, that turned out well. The judge really came through on sentencing."

"Yes, Uncle Aleister is always fair-minded."

They rode downstairs in the elevator, then exited the courthouse to discover light snow falling from a fair sky. Dru stuck out her tongue and caught a few flakes. "I love the snow," she said. "It doesn't snow in Gehenna."

"I should think not," said Leery. "It would ruin Luci's reputation if it did."

They walked toward where they'd left their car half-on and half-off the sidewalk. Dru walked around to the driver's seat. "I'll drop you at your place," she said. "Unless..."

"I really think it would be best," said Leery. "We have to face facts, Dru. I loved having you nearby in Gehenna, but this is Manhattan, and the rules..."

"I understand," said Dru in a small voice.

As she drove to the Upper West Side, Dru seemed lost in thought. Leery, too, didn't have much to say, preferring to lean his head back against the headrest and close his eyes. When Dru pulled up, she found Vinny Gonofrio standing in the door to Leery's building. "Oh, there's Vinny," she said with a little moue. "What's he doing here?"

Leery opened his eyes. "Oh," he said. "We're here." He opened the door, then turned to look at her. "I guess I'll see you later, partner."

She nodded once, dropping her gaze. "Okay."

Though it hurt him to do so, Leery left it there and got out. He watched as Dru pulled away, noticing the slump of her shoulders, the set of her jaw. He was a detective, after all. Then he turned and smiled at Vinny. "Thanks for coming."

"You bet," said Gonofrio. "She doesn't know, does she?" His gaze flicked toward the street.

"No," said Leery. "Not a thing."

Gonofrio shrugged. "If that's how you want to play it."

"Come on, Vinny. Let's get busy."

"How do you want to do it?"

"I figure most of the stuff I could hand you off the balcony and you can fly down. It's probably easier and faster than messing with the elevator."

Gonofrio's wings appeared behind him. "Sure, I'm game." With two beats of his wings, he rose to hover above the sidewalk. "Race you!" Without waiting for a reply, he began to ascend.

"That's hardly fair," shouted Leery, then he turned and dashed inside.

2

The clock in her living room had just struck nine when there was a knock at her door. Dru rose and plodded toward the double doors. She hadn't changed from her work clothes. In fact, she hadn't done anything but sit on the couch and stare morosely out the window. She opened the door without looking through the peephole.

"Hey, Dru-baby," said Leery.

"What..." Dru shook her head. "Hi, Leery. Come on in."

They went into the living room and sat on the couch. "I really love this view," said Leery.

Dru glanced at him, but he wasn't looking at her, and her heart ached a little. Instead, he was staring out at the skyline. "Yes," she said. "It's beautiful at this time of day."

"It really is," he said with a vague sort of smile. "I mean, just look at it."

"I've seen it," she said. A lump formed in her throat, and the thoughts of leaving the police force that had plagued her all afternoon revisited her with a vengeance. "I... Leery, I think we need to talk."

"Shh, Dru-baby. Look at the skyline, would you?"

"I..." She puffed out her cheeks with a big sigh but then looked. A slow smile blossomed, and her eyes sparkled with happy tears. "You're a jerk, Leery Oriscoe." Outside her window, Vinny Gonofrio hovered, smiling and holding a sign that read. "Howdy, neighbor. Please join me for dinner. I'm one floor down. Happy Yule from your new neighbor, L." Dru turned and threw her arms around Leery's neck.

"I would've said Merry Christmas, but I know how you feel about the holiday. I hope Yule is okay."

Dru nodded without pulling away from the hug. "Did you really move in downstairs?"

"I wouldn't lie to you, Dru."

"And, um, is Vinny coming to dinner?"

"Are you kidding?" said Leery. "I want you all to myself."

"Then it's a deal."

Her hot breath tickled his throat, and Leery shivered. "Oh, I should also tell you something."

"What's that, Leery?"

"I hung the mistletoe."

"That will certainly be convenient." Eyes dancing, Dru grinned at him, then pulled him up. As they turned toward the door, Leery waved, and Vinny grinned from ear-to-ear, then turned and flew away.

I hope this novel made you laugh, and that you loved every minute of it. To be one of the first to know what comes next, please consider joining my Readers Group by visiting https://ehv4.us/join. Or follow me on BookBub by visiting my profile page there: https://ehv4.us/bbub.

For my complete bibliography, please visit: https://ehv4.us/bib.

Books these days succeed or fail based on the strength of their reviews. I hope you will consider leaving a review—as an independent author, I could use your help. It's easy (I promise). You can leave your review by clicking on this link: https://ehv4.us/2revcw9

AUTHOR'S NOTE

Ah... It feels good to finish this ninth *CLAW & WARDER* title. It's the ninth in one year, and, of course, I also wrote *Wrath Child* this year (which Supergirl recently informed me is the best thing I've ever written). So summing all those words, and adding in the short fiction I wrote and published, I've published just over 550,000 words this year. That brings me very close to the one-million-word mark for the past two years, which is, you know, *insane,* considering all the "love" Petunia has thrown at me during that time.

When I decided to beat my Personal Monster™ (aka Petunia) in the face by spending my time writing fiction, I made the conscious decision to do it as an indie. Part of my reasoning is that "there are no deadlines" to self-publishing, and that would make it an easier thing to do. Then, I happily went about setting deadlines for myself that have some of my healthy author friends shaking their heads and calling me a machine.

Yeah. I'm smart like that.

Petunia decided I needed a reminder of who was in charge of this boat ride. In suffering through his reminder, I also remembered that "there are no deadlines" lie. I mean, that "there are no deadlines" rule.

There's a voice inside my head right this very minute that's saying, "You did 550,000 words this year...why not go for a million next year?" Pardon me a moment, while I go bang my head against the wall.

Ah, that's better!

But let me talk about *why*. I get asked a lot of the same questions over and over. How do you do it? Why do you write? Aren't you tempted to just sit back and enjoy not having anything to stress you out?

Let me answer them in reverse order because I'm tired and don't want to move the questions around. 'Kay? 'Kay.

I am not tempted by the prospect of sitting back and letting the world float by. I tried that. It made me miserable, and to be honest, it is boring as hell. Life requires participation to make it fun. I write because it is *fun*. I write because I decided several years ago that Petunia can sit and spin. Writing, to me, is like Gandalf standing on that thin bridge of rock and yelling, "You shall not pass!" It's also a balm—it gets my mind off whatever is hurting and lets me jump into a world that I (mostly) can control. Yeah, there are times I curse the self-imposed deadlines. And, I'll be honest, I always curse the business aspects of writing (marketing, bookkeeping, blah).

So, by my count, all that's left is to answer the how question. Mostly, with smoke and mirrors. Nah. It's work, and a lot of it, but I'll tell you a secret my grandfather (the original Hank™) told me when I was much younger. The trick to life is figuring out what you love to do, then finding a way to get paid for doing it. I'm still working on that last part, but the first part of Grandpa's advice I've got nailed. It only took me close to fifty years and a debilitating illness to take that part to heart.

Writing, when you really enjoy it, when you can get past all the bullshit your own mind tries to throw in the way, comes down to time. If you put in the time, you will be rewarded with words.

So, there you go. That's how I do it: I put in the time. What's more, I (mostly) enjoy every second of that time.

I hope you enjoy the results!

So, what will next year bring? I'm not sure yet. I have to check in with my partner (Petunia) and see how much he's willing to let me push. Or if there's a med that makes him shut the hell up.

Will I have another crazy publication schedule? Probably. But I may not tell you about it, so I can pretend I'm not missing deadlines. I do know this: there will be more books.

Lots of them. And I'm going to start writing them next week!

ABOUT THE
AUTHOR

Erik Henry Vick is an author of dark speculative fiction who writes despite a disability caused by his Personal Monster™ (also known as an autoimmune disease.) He writes to hang on to the few remaining shreds of his sanity.

He lives in Western New York with his wife, Supergirl; their son; a Rottweiler named after a god of thunder; and two extremely psychotic cats. He fights his Personal Monster™ daily with humor, pain medicine, and funny T-shirts.

Erik has a B.A. in Psychology, an M.S.C.S., and a Ph.D. in Artificial Intelligence. He has worked as a criminal investigator for a state agency, a college professor, a C.T.O. for an international software company, and a video game developer.

He'd love to hear from you on social media:

Blog: https://erikhenryvick.com
Twitter: https://twitter.com/BerserkErik
Facebook: https://fb.me/erikhenryvick
Amazon author pages:
    USA: https://ehv4.us/amausa
    UK: https://ehv4.us/amauk
Goodreads Author Page: https://ehv4.us/gr
BookBub Author Profile: http://ehv4.us/bbub

Made in the USA
Monee, IL
29 January 2023